The *Alden All Stars* series:

Power Play

ALDEN ALL STARS

Power Play

David Halecroft

VIKING

VIKING
Published by the Penguin Group
Penguin Books USA Inc., 375 Hudson Street, New York, New York 10014, U.S.A.
Penguin Books Ltd, 27 Wrights Lane, London W8 5TZ, England
Penguin Books Australia Ltd, Ringwood, Victoria, Australia
Penguin Books Canada Ltd, 10 Alcorn Avenue, Toronto, Ontario, Canada M4V 3B2
Penguin Books (N.Z.) Ltd, 182–190 Wairau Road, Auckland 10, New Zealand
Penguin Books Ltd, Registered Offices: Harmondsworth, Middlesex, England

First published in 1990 by Puffin Books, a division of Penguin Books USA Inc.
First hardcover edition published in 1992 by Viking, a division of Penguin Books USA Inc.

1   3   5   7   9   10   8   6   4   2

Library of Congress Cataloging-in-Publication Data
Halecroft, David. Power play / by David Halecroft.   p.   cm.—(Alden All Stars)
Summary: Seventh grader Derrick Larson is good enough at hockey to play
on the eighth grade team, but if he does he will leave his friends behind.
I S B N   0 - 6 7 0 - 8 4 6 9 8 - 8
[1. Hockey—Fiction. I. Title. II. Series.
[PZ7.H13825Po 1992 [Fic]—dc20   92-12605 CIP AC

The author also writes as "Joe M. Hudson."
Printed in U.S.A.   Set in Century Schoolbook

Power Play

1

It happened so fast that Woody Franklin didn't know what hit him.

Woody was lined up at center ice with a blond-haired boy he had never seen before. The boy was tall—the tallest on the ice—with piercing blue eyes that seemed to burn holes in the face-off spot. The rest of Alden Junior High's seventh grade hockey team was crouched in ready position, waiting for the very first scrimmage of the year to begin. Woody was watching to see what this boy was all about. He had looked confident during the warm-up drills, but Woody knew you couldn't tell about a hockey player until you saw him handle the puck.

"Okay, boys, let's see your stuff," Coach McKibben said as he skated up to center ice.

Coach threw the puck into the face-off spot. As soon as the puck touched the ice, the new boy took a swing at Woody's stick and whacked it out of position. Before Woody knew what happened, the boy flicked the puck between Woody's legs, skated around him, and picked up the puck on the other side.

This kid was like a whirlwind on the ice. He broke through Josh Bank and Sam Kruger—the two defensemen—and left them in a shower of ice shavings. Woody turned around just in time to see him skating toward the goal in a clean breakaway.

And now the only thing between the new boy and an easy goal was a hundred and sixty pounds of blubber named Bannister.

Since Bannister was fat—and took up a big part of the net just by standing there—Coach had decided to put him in at goalie. He was also the team clown, famous for his lack of coordination. If he was going to lose his balance and fall down all the time, he might as well fall down in front of the goal—where he stood an outside chance of blocking a shot.

The new boy was striding easily toward the goal, all alone, stickhandling the puck in front of him. When he raised his stick for a slap shot, Bannister screamed and covered his face mask with his arm— a typical Bannister move.

The sound of the slap shot echoed like a rifle shot in the Cranbrook Municipal Rink.

The shot looked textbook perfect. It was headed where every coach told you to place your shots— toward the corner of the net, on the goalie's stick side.

But the puck deflected off of the post and went flying over the boards, high into the dark bleachers.

Coach blew the whistle and Bannister brought his arm down from across his face mask.

"Most goalies find it helpful to use their eyes, Bannister," Coach shouted toward the goal.

"But, Coach," Bannister responded, making a face, "I haven't had a goal scored on me *all year!*"

Everyone laughed at Bannister's joke, since "all year" meant approximately the last seven seconds.

The new, blond-haired boy joined in the laughter as he sped back toward center ice. He skated in long swift strides, like a pro.

"Great playing, Derrick," Coach said to the new boy. "Everyone, I'd like you to meet Derrick Larson."

Derrick Larson couldn't believe he had missed his first slap shot of the year . . . especially when the goalie was covering his eyes. Slap shots were his specialty, and that one should have been a cakewalk. He had to admit he was feeling a little rusty today. And the Alden Panthers—his new team—were hardly challenging him to play his best.

Seventh grade was the first year that the junior high schools in Cranbrook had organized hockey teams, and for most of the boys this scrimmage was the first time they had ever *really* played the game. During the drills, Derrick had noticed that his new teammates lacked certain hockey fundamentals. Most of them were good one-way skaters—crossing the right foot over the left—but only Woody Franklin and Sam Kruger could skate well two-way. A good hockey player had to skate well two-way, and he also had to skate backward as well as he skated forward.

As Derrick lined up with Woody for the second face-off of the year, he figured that Woody would try to get him back by going for *his* stick. And he was exactly right. As soon as Coach dropped the puck, Derrick lifted his stick and Woody took a big whiff into thin air. Derrick flipped the puck between

Woody's legs, skated around him, and then charged off with the puck.

It seemed like the same thing all over again. Another whirlwind on ice.

"Sam and Josh, drop back and defend the goal!" Coach yelled.

Josh Bank, one of the defensemen, was an energetic guy whose personality was as fiery red as his bright red hair. Josh had a perfect runner's body—thin and wiry. In fact, Josh was the big hope of Alden's track team. But he looked funny on the ice, kind of like a scarecrow in hockey pads.

As Derrick charged forward, Josh tried to knock the puck away from him with a poke check. But Derrick shifted his stick, and Josh lunged forward onto the ice, face first. He stood up a second later and whacked his stick against the ice in frustration.

Who is this guy? Josh wondered, as he watched Derrick Larson speed out of range.

Derrick felt the awesome power of puck control. His skates seemed to float on the ice and his legs felt like two powerful pistons. Whenever he felt like that, he knew that nothing could stop him.

Nothing.

The other defenseman, a small boy named Sam

Kruger, dropped back and waited for Derrick in the middle of the attacking zone. It was one-on-one.

Sam skated backward, poking his stick out to check Derrick. All Derrick had to do now was fake this guy out, and the goalie wouldn't stand a chance.

Derrick faked like he was going left, and Sam played right into his hands. Just as Sam committed himself to the left, Derrick shoved off to the right and zipped around him.

"Come out of the goal and get the puck, Bannister. Let's see some hustle," Coach McKibben yelled to the boy in the goal.

That's right, goalie, come on out, Derrick thought, as he surged forward toward the goal. *Nothing you can do is going to stop me from scoring now.*

Bannister suddenly came out of the crease, waving his stick and screaming like a savage. His weak ankles were caving in comically. With his white face mask and his bulky pads, Bannister looked like some weird fat droid from outer space.

Derrick wasn't fazed by Bannister's act. He made a fast wrist shot toward the corner of the net, and then cut sharp as Bannister barrelled toward him.

The shot went wide of the goal. Derrick couldn't believe it. It was the first practice of the year, and he was sure he could feel his skills already slipping.

Last year, Derrick thought, *I would have made that shot in a second.*

Coach blew the whistle and the team skated slowly toward center ice.

"Good effort," Josh Bank said as he skated by Derrick. "You're a pretty good skater."

"I used to be better," Derrick mumbled to himself.

"Are you new in school?" Josh asked. "I haven't seen you around."

"I moved to Cranbrook two days ago," Derrick responded.

"Hey, do you guys hear that groovy accent?" Bannister said, half-skating, half-stumbling toward the group of boys at center ice. Bannister had his own vocabulary, and "groovy" was one of his all-time favorite words. He took off his face mask and a big, sweaty, smiling face appeared.

"Leave the mask on and spare us your face," Woody Franklin muttered.

"Or leave the mask off for good," Josh answered. "A few hard slap shots might *improve* your face."

"You guys are a couple of regular comedians," Bannister said, almost falling into the group of boys. He was used to his friends' good-natured ribbing. He even seemed to enjoy it.

"What accent are you talking about, Bannister?" Woody asked.

"This new guy's accent," Bannister said, nodding toward Derrick. "Listen to him talk and tell me if he doesn't have the grooviest Canadian accent you've ever heard."

Derrick looked down at his skates and blushed.

"I'm not from Canada," Derrick said. "I'm from Minnesota."

"Close enough for us," Bannister remarked. "All I know is that you sound like a genuine *hockey* player. Not like this bunch of pansies."

"At least us 'pansies' keep our eyes open when we play," Josh commented under his breath. Everyone laughed.

But the team fell silent as Coach skated up to center ice. Coach McKibben was the gym teacher at Alden, who had been recruited to coach seventh-grade hockey. He was a dedicated fan of the game, even though he had never played himself. He knew hockey well, but he wasn't exactly sure how to coach it.

"All right, men," Coach began. "I can tell we have a lot of work to do this season. First of all: Josh, try to stay on your skates."

A little ripple of laughter went through the group of boys. Coach ignored it and continued talking.

"The rule of thumb is this: your hockey playing is

only as good as your skating. So *all* of you need to work on your skating. Second of all: Woody, Derrick just plain outsmarted you at the face-off. He knew you'd go for his stick—so he lifted it, you whiffed, and the puck was his. That's heads-up hockey, men. And the third thing is . . . Bannister."

Once again a ripple of laughter went through the boys.

"What I said was, 'Bannister, come out of the goal and take the puck.' I didn't say, 'Bannister, come out of the goal and scream and wave your arms and make the new kid in town think he's just moved to Mars.' "

Everyone laughed except Derrick. A deep red blush spread across Derrick's face, and for a second he thought he *had* moved to Mars. He hadn't made a single friend in Cranbrook yet. All of the faces on the hockey team were new and strange. The houses and streets of Cranbrook were new and strange, too. The day before, he had actually gotten *lost* on his way home from school.

If the Alden Panthers had been a better hockey team, then at least he would have felt at home on the ice. But now, even the *ice* felt new and strange.

Yes, thought Derrick sadly, *I have moved to Mars.*

All the boys started skating around the rink, but Coach called Derrick to the sidelines. They sat on the bench and Coach gave Derrick a bunch of information sheets to fill out, and some medical forms to take home to his parents. As Derrick filled in the answers, he watched the Alden Panthers skate around the rink. These guys sure weren't as good as his old team back in Minnesota. If *he* were the coach, Derrick would have had the team do figure eights instead of skate straight around the boards. Then they could at least work on becoming two-way skaters.

After a few minutes, Coach McKibben blew his whistle.

"All right, men, that's the practice," he called out. "And hurry off the ice. The eighth grade team has the rink now."

All the boys skated off the rink, laughing and talking.

"Have those forms filled out for me by tomorrow," Coach said to Derrick as he skated toward the locker room.

The sound of the team's laughter echoed in the rink, and then faded away. Suddenly Derrick was alone, and the little Cranbrook Municipal Rink seemed very big, very cold, and very empty. Derrick would have given a million dollars if he could disappear right then—and reappear magically in Minnesota. He missed his old rink, with its fancy new lights and bright pink Zamboni. He missed his old neighborhood. He missed his old bedroom, with its view of the pine trees and the pond. But most of all he missed his friends, all of the guys he had played with on his old hockey team. They were far, far away.

Derrick could hardly believe it when he felt the hot tears in his eyes. He couldn't really be *crying*, could he? He hadn't cried in years.

Just then the eighth grade team skated out onto the ice. Derrick wiped his eyes and headed off toward the lockers all alone.

2

When his father was transferred to Cranbrook, Derrick Larson had thought that the world would come to an end. It was bad enough to leave all his friends behind. It was bad enough to leave all the neighborhood ponds he used to play hockey on, and the local woods with their secret paths and forts. But when Mr. Larson told him that Cranbrook didn't have a strong hockey program, Derrick had felt that his most cherished hopes and dreams were being crushed.

Derrick had always dreamed of someday playing center on the Minnesota North Stars. Everyone who watched Derrick on the ice could see that he had genuine talent, and that his dream of playing in the NHL wasn't really as crazy as it seemed. He had been the star of his old team, back in Minnesota, and had led them to two league championships. He was a brilliant skater and shooter, excellent on both offense and defense. He could even tend the goal like an expert. With the right coaching, dedicated practice—and the right kind of stiff competition—there was no telling how far Derrick Larson could go.

But Derrick wondered how he could hope to improve his skills in a new, strange school that didn't have a strong hockey program. His first day of practice with the Alden Panthers had confirmed his worst fears.

"Dad, I might as well just forget about being a hockey player," Derrick said that night. "I might as well go ahead and sell my skates and take up tiddlywinks."

He was sitting on the bed in his new room, surrounded by big moving boxes filled with clothes and books. Derrick hadn't had the heart to unpack yet—unpacking would have meant that he was staying in Cranbrook for good. The only things Derrick had taken out of the boxes were his hockey trophies from Minnesota, and his hockey posters— which were already taped all over the walls. Mr. Larson—a tall man with graying sideburns, and eyes as blue as Derrick's—looked at his son knowingly.

"Are the Panthers really that bad, Derrick?" he asked.

"Well, they sure aren't as good as my old team," Derrick answered. "A couple of them don't even know how to skate backward. The goalie's a really funny guy and all, but he covered up his eyes when I took a slap shot."

Mr. Larson chuckled. He had told Derrick a thousand times that the most important player on a hockey team is the goalie. A team with a good goalie stood a chance of victory.

"I swear, Dad, I've already started to play down to their level," Derrick continued. "I had two easy shots on goal that I missed completely. Last year that never would have happened."

"What about the boys on the team?" Mr. Larson asked. "Do you like them?"

"I don't know and I don't care," Derrick said. "I just wish I could go back to Minnesota."

"Well, your feelings may change once you start to

make friends with some of the boys," Mr. Larson pointed out.

Derrick wasn't in the mood for any of his father's words of wisdom. Didn't his father know that hockey—and hockey alone—was the most important thing in Derrick's life?

When his father finally left the room Derrick took down all his trophies, shined them till they sparkled, and wished he could be back in Minnesota with all the friends he had left behind.

At practice the next day, Coach McKibben had the team do shooting drills. Bannister was still in the goal, and it was a sorry sight to watch him slip and slide around, and cower in the net whenever it was Derrick's turn to shoot. Derrick noticed that Woody Franklin—a quiet, medium-sized boy with brown hair—had a pretty good shot. Even red-haired Josh Bank, who was kind of scrawny, could really bear down on a slap shot.

But most of the guys still couldn't skate two-way— and Derrick knew that it didn't matter how well you could shoot, if you couldn't skate yourself into good position.

Derrick wanted to mention this to Coach—but on the other hand, he didn't want to seem too cocky. So at break, when everyone else was eating an orange for energy, Derrick went out onto the ice and began to do big figure eights, skating smoothly behind the goals and back out through center ice. It was a drill his old team had always done, and Derrick did it smoothly—left leg over the right, then right leg over the left.

After three or four figure eights, Coach McKibben called Derrick to the sidelines.

"Derrick, what's that drill for?" he asked.

"It's an old drill to teach you how to skate two-way," Derrick answered.

"It's a good drill," Coach said. "You don't mind if I use it, do you?"

After break, Coach asked Derrick to lead the whole team in figure eights.

Maybe this team can improve, Derrick thought as he skated. *And maybe I can improve, too.*

His high hopes faded as soon as the scrimmage began, though. Derrick dominated the play, stealing the puck, outskating the defensemen, passing well— but no matter how hard he tried, he couldn't get the puck into the net. Not even against Bannister.

At a stop in the action, Derrick decided it was time for him to score a spectacular goal. Back in Minnesota, he had been the league's top scorer and had been known for his amazing slap shot. Derrick knew that if he tried to hit the puck too hard, he might lose control. But he didn't care, he was going to rip a killer shot, one so hard it would burn a hole through the net.

As soon as play started up again, Woody—who was on Derrick's team today—brought the puck over the blue line and passed it to Derrick, who sped forward along the boards. Sam Kruger was sweep-checking him, but Derrick faked Sam and cut around to the left. Woody was in perfect position to receive a pass at the net, but Derrick wanted to prove himself with a shot on goal. He wound up, even though he wasn't in the best shooting position, and blasted a cannon slap shot. His awesome power sent the puck screaming forward.

But the puck flew about fifteen feet over Bannister's head, and landed halfway up the bleachers.

Derrick skated back toward center ice with a dazed and crestfallen face.

"Derrick, why don't you ease off a bit," Coach said. "Guys your age have a hard time handling all that power."

I never had a hard time handling all that power before I moved to Cranbrook, Derrick thought sadly.

Everyone had to admit that Bannister was improving in the goal. On one shot he even saved a

goal by catching the puck in his goaltender's mitt—
and the whole team burst into wild applause. Bannister removed his face mask and took a long dra-
matic bow.

"Okay, Mr. Hollywood," Coach said, smiling.
"Let's see if you can do a repeat performance."

Toward the end of the scrimmage, Derrick was
fore-checking behind the goal line, working A.J.
Pape into the boards. A.J. lost control of the puck
and Derrick stickhandled it up the left wing board,
skating hard and then breaking suddenly toward
the goal. He was sure he could see Bannister's pads
shaking with fear.

Derrick was aiming for the corner of the net, but
instead he hit Bannister square in the stomach with
a vicious slap shot. Bannister made the save but
went down gasping on the ice.

Coach blew the whistle and the whole team
crowded around the goal.

Bannister was fine. He had just had the wind
knocked out of him. Still, he was pretty shaken up,
and it was clear that he would not be getting back
into net at *this* practice.

"Derrick, suit up," Coach said.

"Me?" Derrick asked, hoping it wasn't true. "You
want *me* to play goalie?"

"Go out and give it your best," Coach answered. "We'll finish off with some shot practice."

The goalie's pads felt heavy and strange on Derrick as he skated toward the goal. He knew that the goalie was the most important player on the ice, but still . . . he loved playing center, taking slap shots, scoring game-winning goals. Mr. Larson had played goalie, and he had taught Derrick everything he knew about goaltending. So when Derrick reached the crease, he turned, flexed his knees, lifted his goaltender's mitt, and set his thick goalie's stick on the ice before him—just like a pro.

Nobody could score. Derrick's reactions were lightning fast. Woody charged him and sent a smoldering slap shot to his stick side, but Derrick made a beautiful kick save, deflecting the puck off his leg pad. Josh made a perfect flip shot up into the far corner, but Derrick dove and caught it in his goaltender's mitt. Having Derrick in the crease was like having a brick wall in front of the net.

After practice, Derrick was sitting on the sidelines removing his pads when Woody skated up to him.

"You're pretty good in the goal," Woody said, smiling.

"Thanks," Derrick answered.

"Matter of fact, you're pretty good on offense, too,"

Woody continued. "And did I mention defense? Welcome to the Alden Panthers. And, boy, do we need you."

Derrick looked up and smiled.

"Enough of the Panthers," Woody said. "Practice is over till tomorrow. What you need now is a tour of Cranbrook, a slice of pizza, and a few video games over at the Game Place."

Just then, Josh Bank skated up and made a double-leg stop, spraying the boards with ice.

"Hurry out of those things, Derrick," Josh exclaimed. "We've got some pizza to eat!"

3

"You're crazy if you think Gordie Howe was the best player of all time," Woody exclaimed, as he chewed a huge bite of pizza. "Gretzky dominates!"

"I'm not saying that Gretzky hasn't scored more goals," Derrick responded, smiling and taking a gulp of soda. "I'm only saying that nobody was as fun to watch as Gordie Howe."

The three boys were sitting in a booth at Pete's Pizza later that afternoon, laughing and talking. Paper plates and napkins and cups were strewn all over the table.

"I don't mean to be a party pooper, Derrick," Josh commented, "but you weren't even *born* when Gordie Howe was playing. So how do *you* know what he played like?"

"My dad has tapes of all the great players," Derrick answered. "You guys should come over sometime and watch them. It's totally amazing."

"Nothing's as totally amazing as watching Bannister," Josh said, rolling his eyes. "Except maybe watching Pee-wee Herman."

The boys laughed.

"Yeah, I wonder why Coach is playing him at goalie," Woody said. "It seems like kind of an important position."

"Bannister's the perfect goalie. You know why?" Derrick remarked, with a little smirk. "Because he's four feet tall and five feet wide. He fits right into the net."

Everyone laughed, and Derrick took his last bite of pizza. There was only one slice left on the plate.

"Who gets the last slice?" Woody asked. "I'm still starving."

"Let's face off for it," Derrick suggested.

"I'll officiate," Josh answered, springing to his feet.

So Josh, with his impish eyes gleaming, pushed the plate into the middle of the table. Woody and Derrick stood up and got ready. They each put their hands at their sides and tried to hold back their laughter as Josh lifted the pizza slice high above the table.

"Okay, gentlemen, let's see what you can do," Josh said, imitating Coach's voice.

Josh dropped the slice of pizza and as soon as it hit the plate, two hands shot out from either side to grab it. All three of them were laughing like crazy as Derrick and Woody tore the pizza in two, and shoved what they had into their mouths. As they stood there laughing, they looked like two chipmunks with their cheeks stuffed.

"No hard feelings?" Woody responded, offering Derrick his hand, which was covered with pizza sauce.

"Shake your own hand," Derrick answered, laughing. "That's the oldest trick in the book."

After they left Pete's Pizza, the three boys walked next door to the Game Place. In the middle of the floor, surrounded by all the noisy video games, was a big, solitary Stanley Cup hockey game. Josh and Woody had been playing on this board for so many years that they knew exactly how fast each player could flip the little plastic puck, and which knobs were stiff or bent. But they pretended they'd never seen the game in all their lives.

"Hey, let's try this game," Josh said, winking secretly at Woody.

"Great! I used to have a Stanley Cup game like this when I was a kid," Derrick said, as he set himself up behind the board.

Derrick challenged Josh, and the game lasted about thirty seconds. Derrick didn't even get a shot on goal. The final tally was 10–0.

"You're pretty good, Josh," Derrick said, stunned.

"Better than he is on the real ice," Woody commented.

Derrick had to admit that his pride was a little shaken by the quick defeat. It was only an arcade game, but still . . . it *was* hockey. And if it was hockey, then he should win.

"Let me have a try at Woody," Derrick said.

That game was even shorter than the first. The final score was 10–0.

"Am I really that bad?" Derrick said as they walked out into the brisk autumn evening.

"Let's put it this way, Derrick," Josh commented. "You do a whole lot better on *real* ice."

"I don't know about that," Derrick said, with a note of doubt in his voice. "I used to be better. I couldn't even score a goal against *Bannister* today. I swear I can feel my skills slipping since I left Minnesota. I mean, nothing against the team, or anything."

"It may be bad for *you*," Woody said, patting Derrick on the back. "But having you on the team sure as heck is good for *us*."

"You better believe it," Josh said. "Welcome aboard."

The three boys walked all over Cranbrook—down Main Street, through Danahy's woods, and past Black's Pond where a few boys were skating. Now that Derrick was discovering the town, he was beginning to like it. By the time the boys had finished with their grand tour of Cranbrook, the sky was growing dark.

Derrick said good-bye to his new friends at the turnoff to his street. As he walked home, he felt a strange new feeling. He suddenly kind of liked his new street. And when he turned into his driveway, his new green house didn't seem so bad.

After dinner Derrick ran upstairs and unpacked all of his boxes. It seemed like it was finally time to settle down in Cranbrook. After an hour of work, Derrick's room looked like he had lived in it for all of his twelve years.

Later that night, when Derrick was finishing up some homework, Mr. Larson knocked on the door. He came into Derrick's room holding a hockey stick and a carton of eggs.

"Did you have a good day?" Mr. Larson asked, smiling.

"Yeah, I met some nice guys on the team," Derrick said. "We went out for pizza, and then they beat my pants off in a game of arcade hockey. I can't even seem to play *that* well."

"Derrick, I know you're worried about your skills," Mr. Larson said. "But I know a simple drill that will help you keep your stickhandling up to snuff."

Mr. Larson set one egg down on Derrick's hardwood floor.

"All you have to do is stickhandle the egg back and forth," Mr. Larson said, demonstrating. "If you break the egg, you're not using enough finesse. And finesse is the name of the game."

Mr. Larson handed the stick and egg to his son with a smile.

"Thanks, Dad," Derrick said.

"And by the way, Derrick, your room looks great," Mr. Larson said, winking. "I'm glad you've decided to stay."

As soon as his father left, Derrick jumped up from his chair and tried the drill. By the time he went to bed, he had broken half a dozen eggs—but it was worth it, if he could keep up his hockey skills.

4

"Listen up, men, I've got some important things to say," Coach McKibben exclaimed at the beginning of practice the next day. "Number one. We've got our first game next Wednesday, against Williamsport, and we're still a little ragged on the ice. Williamsport is not a pushover squad. If we're going to win, we're going to have to *work*. Understand?"

Coach was standing on the ice, holding a clipboard, while the whole Alden Panther squad sat on the bench. It was the day when Coach was announcing the positions, and the team was dead silent.

Derrick wished Coach would hurry through his big speech and get to the announcements. He was almost sure he'd get the position he wanted: center on the first line.

"Now let me tell you something about the game of hockey, men," Coach said, looking at the boys with serious eyes. "Hockey is not won on offense. Hockey is not won with big rocket slap shots from the blue line. Hockey is won on *defense*. Hear me? Our team motto should be: Score if you can, but above all make sure the other team *doesn't* score."

Derrick had to agree with everything Coach was saying. He had heard his father say the same thing a hundred times. But the truth was, defense just wasn't as much *fun* as offense. Derrick had played center on his old team in Minnesota—and that was the position he knew and loved. He loved being the playmaker, and taking those rocket slap shots from the blue line.

"Every coach is tempted to take the player who's the worst skater, the worst shooter, and put him in the goal," Coach continued. "This is the worst thing a coach can do. The goalie is the most important player on the team, even though he doesn't get a lot of glory."

Derrick started to get a bad feeling in his gut. He

thought he could feel what Coach was working up to. But he didn't want to think about it.

"In fact, the goalie needs to be an excellent skater, and an excellent stickhandler," Coach McKibben said. "It's the hardest and most important position on the ice. A smart coach will put his *best* player in the goal."

Josh nudged Derrick with his elbow.

"And so, Derrick, I want you to play goalie this year."

Derrick's heart fell. He sat on the bench in shock, and didn't even listen to the rest of Coach's speech. Coach said that Josh and Woody and A.J. Pape would be on the first-team front line, with Woody as center, Josh as left wing, and A.J. as right wing. On the second-team front line would be Bill Fitzpatrick and Dave McShea and Alex Kroll. The first-team defensemen would be Sam Kruger and Russell Schultz. The second-team defensemen would be Bannister and John Lilly.

"Now I want you to get out there and do Derrick's famous figure eight drill," Coach said at last. "And I want you to really *concentrate* on skating both ways. Okay, go to it, men."

As the rest of the team poured out onto the ice, Derrick sat alone on the sidelines, slowly putting on the goalie's pads. He knew it was the right decision for the team . . . but still. He couldn't believe he was going to play goalie. It felt like the final blow to his dream of someday playing center on the Minnesota North Stars.

Coach started off with some shot practice.

Derrick knew that the golden rule of goalkeeping was to play the puck and not the shooter's body. If you played the shooter's body, you were likely to get faked, commit yourself too early, and leave the net open for an easy goal.

But it seemed like the Panthers had never even *heard* of a fake. All they did was rush and shoot, and Derrick kept his eye on the puck and easily made the saves. After ten minutes of the drill, Derrick was already getting bored and frustrated. So to make his new job more fun, he decided to try all the different goaltending techniques his father had taught him.

The hardest one was the butterfly drop, which required perfect timing. When Derrick saw the puck was coming in low, he would drop to his knees, so that his pads laid like a butterfly's wings along the ice. Then he would put his stick in front of the gap between his knees. As long as he went down in time to get his pads on the ice, he would never let a shot go by.

Power Play

He did the full split, the half split, and the kick
save. He dipped his pads and stacked his pads and
did the inside pad dip. He caught with his goaltender's mitt and blocked with his blocker. He made
sure that he cushioned every shot, so that the puck
wouldn't rebound off his pads or stick and back into
the other team's possession.

He was like a living instructor's manual on goaltending.

As the practice neared the end, a few members of
the eighth grade hockey team came into the rink
and sat in the bleachers. They were all suited up for
their own practice, and were waiting impatiently for
the seventh graders to clear off the ice.

"Look at that hot dog," Mike Rothman, the center
of the eighth grade team, said to his friend. The two
of them sneered and chuckled as they couldn't help
but notice Derrick and his expert goaltending tech-
nique. "He must think he's the coolest."

"There's nothing I hate worse than a little seventh
grader who thinks he's hot stuff," Jason Petrowsky
remarked.

"He does look like hot stuff," said Nick Wilkerson.

"Well, I think we should teach him a little lesson,"
Rothman suggested.

"Yeah, definitely," Petrowsky said.

Their chance came after the practice. Derrick was sitting on the sidelines, taking off his gear, while all of his teammates were in the locker room. Rothman and Petrowsky were warming up with figure eights.

"Nice work, hot dog," Rothman sneered as he skated by.

"Why don't you just leave junior high and join the NHL, big boy," Petrowsky added, spraying Derrick with ice shavings.

The boys burst into laughter.

What's their problem? Derrick wondered. *What did I ever do to them?*

A few minutes later, Derrick, Josh, and Woody were hanging out at the Game Place, talking about that day's practice. Derrick and Josh were in the middle of a game of Stanley Cup hockey.

"What's up with those eighth graders?" Derrick asked, as he saved a shot. "Are they total jerks, or what?"

"They're a bunch of snobs," Woody said.

"Yeah. They've got a great team and it's gone to their heads," Josh commented, as he maneuvered the plastic puck up the board.

"Hey, do you guys think I was being a hot dog at practice today?" Derrick asked.

"No way," Josh answered, shaking his head. "We

just weren't challenging you enough. You were like a brick wall in the goal."

"Yeah, you really made it look easy," Woody said, eyeing Derrick with admiration.

"That's only because you guys *made* it too easy for me," Derrick said, feeling a little better from all the compliments. "You guys have to learn how to deke the goalie."

"What's a deke?" Woody asked.

"A deke is when you fake someone into committing himself and then burn him by going the other way," Derrick answered. "But you can't deke unless you can stickhandle with finesse. Next time we're on the ice, I'll show you some great stickhandling drills from my old team."

"Listen, I've got a great idea, Derrick," Josh said excitedly. "Why don't we get the whole team together this Sunday at Black's Pond, so you can give us some pointers? How does that sound?"

"Why not?" Derrick said. "Sounds like fun."

"Do you really mean it?" Josh said, his eyes glimmering playfully. "Look me in the eyes and say it."

As soon as Derrick lifted his eyes from the board, Josh made a beautiful slap shot from inside the blue line, and the puck landed right in Derrick's goal.

"How's that for a deke, bigshot?" Josh laughed.

The final score was Josh 10, Derrick 3.

5

That Sunday, the whole team met at Black's Pond for a special practice. The pond sat at the edge of the woods, surrounded by trees and a big field of snow. It was a beautiful clear blue day, and the team's spirits were sky-high.

When everyone had shown up, Josh skated out to the center of the pond and called the practice to order.

"Okay, men," he said, smacking his stick against the ice. He looked quite proud of himself and his chest was puffed out a little. "This practice was my idea. Everyone knows that Coach McKibben is a great coach, but sometimes he needs a little help. And Derrick Larson is just the guy to give it. Derrick was the star of a championship team up in Minnesota, which is the hockey capital of the country. He knows some drills that might be able to help us out. We've got our first game coming up on Wednesday, against Williamsport. Williamsport is not a pushover squad, men, and *we* don't even know how to deke the goalie. I bet some of you don't even know what a deke *is!* We need to work on our skating and our stickhandling and our . . ."

"Hey, Josh, if I had known we were getting a sermon, I would have brought some chairs with me," Bannister called out.

Everyone laughed and Josh's chest deflated.

"Why don't you go ahead and do that?" Derrick said, skating up to Bannister with a smile.

"Why don't I do what?" Bannister asked, looking at Derrick skeptically.

"Why don't you go home and bring back some chairs," Derrick said. "Isn't that your house right there?"

"Yeah, that's my house," Bannister responded. "But I don't get the joke."

"It's no joke," Derrick said. "It's a drill. The chair drill, for learning how to stickhandle and deke. Bannister, take John and A.J. and Alex and run over to your house. Bring back eight chairs, any type."

"Why don't we just save ourselves the trouble and bring out a couple of sofas, a TV, a microwave, and sit around on the pond making popcorn and *watching* some groovy hockey on TV?" Bannister said, as he headed off toward his house with the group of boys.

Everyone laughed, and then all eyes turned back to Derrick.

"Okay, men. We've got a lot of work to do," Derrick began. "Now, playing on a pond is a little strange because there are no boards and no lines. But at least the town puts up hockey nets."

"Hey, Derrick," Woody called out, shaking his head. "Guess what Bannister told me the other day? He said he'd never really figured out what all those lines were for anyway."

There was a little bit of laughter around the team . . . but not as much as Derrick had expected. Was it possible that some of the other guys didn't know what the lines were for, either?

"Does everyone here know what the lines are for?"

Everyone nodded, but without much spirit. Derrick rolled his eyes.

"Oh, boy, do we *ever* have some work to do," Derrick said. And then he bent down and etched a little diagram into the ice with his stick.

"The two blue lines and the red center line are used to call offsides and icing," Derrick began. "You are offside when you cross your opponent's blue line *before* the puck crosses it. That means you can't stand next to your opponent's net just waiting for a long pass and an easy goal. Offsides makes you *work* for your breakaways. See?"

Everyone nodded.

"And icing is when you shoot the puck from behind the red line, and it goes all the way past the other team's blue line," Derrick said. "That's to keep you from just whacking the puck up ice and hoping to get it later. Everyone got it?"

They nodded again.

"Good. Now let's warm up with some figure eights," Derrick said, clapping his hands and starting off across the ice with powerful strides.

After a few minutes of figure eights, Bannister and his crew came trudging through the snow with eight chairs. When they got to the pond, Bannister put his chair down, sat on it like a king on his throne, and made John Lilly push him across the ice. But John gave him a huge push and Bannister went speeding and spinning across the pond, screaming and laughing as he went. When the chair hit the ground on the other side, Bannister flew headfirst into the snow.

The whole team broke up in laughter.

Bannister stood up, white with snow from head to foot, and skated across the ice with his back hunched over, making strange noises.

"I'm the Abominable Snowman! Aaaargh!"

"Okay, Mr. Snowman," Derrick said, laughing. "Since you're so terrifying, why don't you set up those chairs in two rows of four, about ten feet apart. I want each of you—including the Abominable Snowman—to work on faking out the chairs. Skate as fast as you can through them, and mix up your moves. Sometimes deke the chair, sometimes put the puck through the legs. Make sure you go to both your forehand and your backhand side. All right, men. Everybody grab a puck and go!"

After about a half hour of instruction, everybody looked better—even the Abominable Snowman. Then it was time to take some shots on goal.

As Derrick crouched down in front of the net, he had to admit that his heart was pounding pretty hard. He wondered if he had wasted everybody's time with his drilling, or whether they had actually learned something.

His question was answered as soon as Woody Franklin charged toward him with the puck. Woody lifted his stick like he was aiming for the right side of the goal, and Derrick made his move to the right. But Woody stopped short and when Derrick was out of position, Woody shot to the left and made an easy goal.

Success! Even though he had given up a goal, Derrick was flooded with happiness, and everyone on the team let out a big cheer. From now on, Derrick would have to be more careful in the net. But that was all right with him—as long as the Panthers were improving.

When the team was getting ready to leave the pond after a good long practice, Derrick noticed six or seven guys from the eighth grade team standing nearby, watching them with smirks on their faces. Derrick recognized Rothman and Petrowsky, the two guys who had heckled him a couple of days earlier. Nick Wilkerson was there also, but he seemed too busy goofing around with Justin Johnson to care about the seventh graders.

"Look at all the big seventh graders," Rothman said as the boys walked by. "Out on the ice doing their fancy chair drills."

"And with their fancy hot dog coach," Petrowsky added with a sneer.

Since the eighth graders were bigger than them, the seventh graders had to ignore their taunts and walk away.

"Those guys drive me nuts," Josh said, as soon as they were out of earshot. His face was turning red. Josh was famous for being hotheaded. "If they don't watch out, I swear I'll . . ."

"You'll make a nice doormat for their front steps, that's what you'll do," Woody answered quickly. "Those guys are twice as big as we are. Derrick's the only one who's their size."

"There is such a thing as *pride,* for your information," Josh responded, hitting his hand into his fist.

"How good is that team, anyway?" Derrick asked.

"They're pretty darn good," Josh admitted. "That's the only reason they can get away with it."

"That and their size," Woody added, elbowing Josh.

By the time the three friends had walked to Derrick's house, met Mr. and Mrs. Larson, and finished a whole tray of brownies, they had forgotten all about the eighth graders. They were talking a mile a minute about the practice on Black's Pond, and Derrick was describing cool plays and sketching diagrams on napkins.

Then Derrick made a mistake: he showed Josh and Woody the egg drill. He should have known it would be a bad combination—three good friends and a dozen eggs. After approximately one minute of serious stickhandling, the egg fight broke out and screams of laughter echoed in the Larsons' basement. The boys came upstairs, completely covered in eggs, with bits of shell still sticking in their hair. They tried hard to keep their faces serious—in case Mrs. Larson got angry. But Mr. and Mrs. Larson couldn't help but laugh. Derrick could tell that his parents liked his new friends. He liked them, too—even as much as the ones he'd left behind in Minnesota.

The only thing that got Derrick a little depressed was talking about the upcoming game against Williamsport. He had almost forgotten that he would be playing goalie.

6

On Wednesday afternoon, the Alden Panthers were riding on the bus to Williamsport. Derrick was sitting in the back with Josh and Woody and A.J. Pape, listening to them talk excitedly about their strategy for the season's first game.

"I hear Williamsport is weak on defense," Woody said. "That means the front line needs to look for opportunities."

"I'll try to get the puck to you as often as I can," A.J. said to Woody. "And try to stay somewhere in front of the net. You're the best shot, and I'm a pretty good passer."

"Don't you guys forget about me," Josh remarked, waving his finger at his friends. "My plan is to sit myself at the left wing point, just over the blue line. If you guys get in trouble, just pass back to me and I'll take a wicked slap shot."

"You couldn't hit the side of a barn with one of your 'wicked slap shots,' " Woody said with a smile. "Leave the slap shots to me."

Derrick tapped his fingers on his goalie's pads as he listened to his friends talk. Why wasn't *he* going to take those big slap shots? Wasn't *he* the best player on the team? Why did *he* have to play goalie? Did Coach want to ruin his entire hockey career?

But Derrick didn't say a word. He knew that it would be best for the team if he played goalie. *Still,* the longer he played goalie on a team like the Panthers, the more his hockey skills would slip.

"Any advice for us, Mr. Goalie?" Woody asked as they pulled up at the Williamsport Ice Rink.

"Only one thing," Derrick answered. "Don't screen me."

"What do you mean?"

"I mean don't stand right in front of me so I can't

see the puck," Derrick said. "If I have to play goalie, I sure as heck don't want to look bad."

But six minutes into the first period, something happened that made Derrick look very bad indeed. And it was exactly what he had warned his friends about.

Williamsport had dominated play in the opening minutes of the game, moving the puck well and fore-checking aggressively. They were getting the puck back from Alden while it was still in Alden's defensive zone—and then they put a lot of pressure on Derrick in the goal. The Williamsport center would steal the puck from an Alden defenseman and pass out to the man at the point, who would take a slap shot at Derrick.

Derrick had made some brilliant saves. One time the puck was flying toward the edge of the net and Derrick made an incredible kick save, flinging up his leg like he was punting a football. The first line defensemen, Sam Kruger and Russell Schultz, were good about staying clear of the crease, so they wouldn't screen Derrick from any shots on goal.

But as soon as Coach changed up the sides, and Bannister and John Lilly were the defensemen, things were completely different. The puck never seemed to leave the Panthers' defensive zone. They never even had a shot on Williamsport's goal.

Six minutes into the first period, the puck got tied up in a big clump of people right in front of the net. Derrick's eyes were wide open and his legs were flexed and ready to spring in any direction. Then Bannister and John Lilly parked themselves right in front of him, completely blocking Derrick's view of the action.

"Hey, Bannister, get out of the way," Derrick called out through his mask. "I can't see a thing."

As he spoke, a weak shot went trickling into the net, right between Derrick's legs. The whole Williamsport rink erupted in applause.

Derrick was humiliated. He had given up a goal . . . and on such a stupid shot!

The score at the end of the first period was Williamsport 1, Alden 0.

At the break, Derrick gave Bannister and Lilly such a solid piece of his mind that, when the next period began, they stayed as far away from the goal as they could. And that was fine with Derrick. As long as he could see the action, he could make the save.

Alden was making lots of silly mistakes, and getting called for every foul from charging to high-sticking. For the whole second period, Alden seemed to keep at least one of its players in the penalty box— and so Williamsport was on a permanent power play.

45

That put the pressure on Derrick. He felt better when Josh and Woody and A.J. were out on the ice. At least those guys could get some action going in the attacking zone, and take the heat off Derrick. But when the second lines were on the ice, Derrick seemed to be making a great save every fifteen seconds.

Somehow, Derrick got through the second period without giving up a goal. But Alden hadn't scored either, so they were still down by one.

Five minutes into the third period, Williamsport was called for charging, but since Alden had possession of the puck, the referee raised his hand for a delayed foul. That meant that as soon as Williamsport touched the puck, the whistle would blow and the charging foul would be called. Derrick knew that a good team takes advantage of a delayed foul. Back in Minnesota, as soon as the ref raised his hand the goalie would have hurried off the ice, and a sixth offensive player would have come on for a fast power play. If Alden had only known, they could have had a one-man advantage, and maybe even scored a goal.

It was a game of lost opportunities. Woody had a clean breakaway toward the end of the third period, and Derrick thought he might even score. But he forgot to deke the goalie. He just wound up and shot straight at him and the goalie caught the puck in his glove.

Another lost opportunity. The final score was Williamsport 1, Alden 0.

"You played a gutsy game, men," Coach said on the bus going home. "You held Williamsport to only one goal. You should be proud."

"If Bannister had been goalie," Josh whispered to Derrick, "Williamsport would have scored about seventy-five goals."

"Too bad Bannister screened you on that one goal," Woody said.

"Yeah, it's too bad," Derrick answered. "But we'll never win if we don't put the puck in the net ourselves."

"I guess our offense was kind of weak, too," Woody said.

Derrick nodded. "I've got some ideas for next Sunday's special practice," he said thoughtfully. "I think I know a few things we can do to help us score next time."

7

"Okay, men, we've had enough of the chair drill," Derrick called out. "Bring it in, and let's talk about how we're going to score some goals against North Colby."

Everyone pushed the chairs off the ice and skated up to Derrick, who was standing in the middle of Black's Pond. This Sunday's special practice seemed to be going even better than the first.

"We missed a lot of great opportunities against Williamsport," Derrick began, once the boys had settled down. "Whenever we had a shot on goal, we seemed to forget that we had ever done the chair drill. We just plain forgot to deke the goalie. We'll never score if we don't fake out the goalie."

"If we do this groovy chair drill for another second, I swear I'll be deking in the halls at school, and deking at the dinner table, and even deking in bed," Bannister said, his big face sweating after the hard drill.

Everyone laughed.

"We won't do the chair drill anymore," Derrick said, with a big smile. "I know another way we can take advantage of opportunities against North Colby. Now, Coach has told us about the power play. That's when we have more men on the ice than the other team, because one of their guys is in the penalty box. That gives us a big advantage, right? The problem is that the ref usually blows the whistle and gives the other team time to get ready for the power play."

"But doesn't the ref always blow the whistle and stop the action when there's a penalty?" Woody asked.

"No, he doesn't," Derrick answered, eyes glimmering with excitement. "See, sometimes he calls a delayed penalty. Like he did against Williamsport.

That means that he won't blow the whistle until the other team gets the puck. Once the other team touches the puck, the play is dead. That means that it's safe for the goalie to leave the ice."

"Oh, yeah," Sam Kruger said. "I've seen the pros do it."

"It's the coolest thing," A.J. said. "And then another player gets on the ice to replace the goalie . . . and you've got yourself a power play."

"Exactly!" Derrick exclaimed. "If we did that in a game, we'd totally surprise the other team. They wouldn't know what hit them! We'd be like the pros."

"So how do we do it?" A.J. asked.

"When the ref raises his arm for a delayed penalty," Derrick began, "I'll come rushing off the ice. But someone on the bench has to be ready to jump in and replace me. How about you, A.J.?"

"You got it," A.J. cried.

"What a great plan!" Josh exclaimed.

"Really cool," Woody said.

Derrick smiled. "I'll talk to Coach about it tomorrow."

"Then on Wednesday let's go out and give North Colby a pounding!" Josh cried.

Team spirit was at an all-time high when the Panthers took the ice on Wednesday. Woody took the face-off, getting the puck out to Josh, who stickhandled away from the defense. Then Woody broke clear and Josh passed the puck just as Woody crossed the blue line. Woody faked out the defenseman and sped toward the goal. He made the goalie think he was going to shoot to the left, but then he stopped and made a wrist shot to the right instead. The North Colby goalie made a beautiful save.

But that was fine. Woody's breakaway had given the Panthers a shot of spirit.

The spirit slowly faded, however, as North Colby took command of the game. North Colby was a good fore-checking squad and most of the action took place around Alden's goal. Toward the end of the period, the action got snarled up around the left boards. Every player on the ice seemed to be bumping into one another and fighting for the puck. Derrick started to get nervous when the big group began drifting toward the goal. In a few seconds all of the action was going on five feet from the net.

Derrick crouched down, alert and ready. He knew he not only had to watch the man, but also to keep his eye on the puck. So when the puck shot out of the pack toward the goal, Derrick saw it coming and dropped onto his pads for a butterfly save.

But at the very last second, the puck deflected off

Josh's skate and took off in a new direction. Derrick tried to get his stick on the puck but he didn't have time. Just as the puck went into the net, the buzzer rang for the end of the first period. Alden was down by a goal.

One encouraging sign was that Alden wasn't fouling nearly as much as they had against Williamsport. In fact, they hadn't sent anyone to the penalty box during the whole first period.

All that changed early in the second period, when Russell Schultz was called for body-checking someone into the boards. Body-checking was illegal in seventh grade hockey. The first year for body-checking in the local league was the eighth grade. So Russell went into the penalty box, and North Colby went on the power play.

North Colby worked the puck into Alden's defensive zone, passing back and forth between the center and the left winger. Sam Kruger was playing a zone defense, covering the slot in front of the goal. Woody was doing a good job keeping the center busy with poke checks, but suddenly the center broke away from him and came speeding toward Sam.

Derrick crouched down and got ready. The center deked Sam and then wound up with a big cannon slap shot.

It was all instinct for Derrick, all pure reaction. He couldn't see the puck at all. His goaltender's glove just flew out on its own and then Derrick felt the impact of the puck. He ended up on the ice before he realized that he had made an unbelievable save.

He jumped back onto his skates and dropped the puck for Woody.

"Get it out of our zone and rag it," he called out.

Woody stickhandled up ice and the Panthers ragged the puck between them—passing it back and forth—until Russell Schultz's penalty was over and Alden was back to full strength.

Pretty good defense . . . but where was Alden's offense?

When the third period started, the score was still 1–0, North Colby. But five minutes later, things had changed.

One of the North Colby players was called for cross-checking. Alden still had the puck, though, so the ref raised his hand for a delayed penalty.

Immediately, Derrick took off speed-skating toward his bench—just like they had planned last Sunday at Black's Pond.

"Just keep possession of the puck," Derrick yelled out to his teammates as he jumped over the boards.

Coach, too, was yelling words of encouragement.

He had welcomed Derrick's suggestion and knew that the other teams would be in for a surprise.

A.J. was ready. As soon as Derrick got off the ice, A.J. jumped on, and Alden was suddenly at a one-man advantage.

Woody was ragging the puck and waiting for A.J. to make a charge. North Colby was confused by the extra man on the ice, and they kept looking to the ref like they expected him to blow the whistle. But as A.J. charged forward, Woody gave him a beautiful pass and cut around his defenseman into open ice. A.J. stickhandled for a split second and then passed back to Woody, who opened up with a blistering slap shot, and put the puck into the top left corner of the net.

Goal!

All of their practice at the pond had paid off. The crowd at the Cranbrook Municipal Rink went crazy.

"That was some heads-up hockey, Derrick," Coach said, beaming a big smile as Derrick skated back toward the goal.

There was only one minute left in the game when the North Colby center took a slap shot from the point and caught Derrick off guard. The puck slipped into the net just under his glove.

The final score was North Colby 2, Alden 1.

Derrick was frustrated about the last goal. He couldn't believe he had given it up. As he and Josh skated off the ice, the guys from the eighth grade team were waiting to rub it in.

"What happened to the hotshot goalie?" Rothman said.

"Is the hotshot goalie crying?" Petrowsky said. "Do I see tears on his little cheeks?"

"No, you don't see tears on his cheeks," Josh said, spinning on Petrowsky. Josh's face was red with anger. "He's better than all you guys put together. Why don't you rats just crawl back into your dirty little holes."

"Those are big words for such a little boy," Rothman said, sneering.

"Someday I swear I'm going to—" Josh began, but Derrick jerked him away and pulled him toward the locker room.

"Don't worry about those jerks," Derrick said.

"But they can't say those kinds of things about *our* star player," Josh answered. "You played a terrific game, Derrick, and they have no right to say anything."   •

"On the other hand," Derrick answered, "I could have done better."

8

Three weeks later, Josh, Woody, Derrick, and Bannister were all sitting in the lunchroom together, talking about the season. The lunchroom was crowded and noisy, and their table was covered with paper bags and cartons of milk. Bannister always ate everybody's leftovers, and he had already collected a little pile of half-eaten sandwiches and cookies in front of him.

"Bannister, if you keep eating like that, you might just *grow* into being a good goalie," Josh said, winking his eye. "All we'd have to do is roll you out in front of the net."

"I happen to have a high metabolism," Bannister answered. "And I wouldn't mind playing goalie, either. It's a lot easier on my ankles."

"I think we've got the best goalie in the league right now," Woody said, nodding to Derrick.

"But that doesn't seem to have helped us much," Derrick said, shrugging. "The season's already a quarter finished and we haven't won a single game."

"That's not your fault," Woody said. "That's the offense's fault. And you really *are* an awesome goalie."

"On the other hand, Derrick is the best skater and shooter on the team, too," Josh said, taking a big bite of his sandwich. "And sometimes I think we should go ahead and put old Bannister back in the goal, just so Derrick can get out and score some goals for us."

"I'd *love* to get out and play offense," Derrick said.

"And then you wouldn't have to worry about losing your hockey skills," Woody added.

"I'm all for it!" Bannister said, shoving an entire half of a ham sandwich into his mouth.

"The three of us would make a great front line," Derrick said to Woody and Josh. "We each know how the other thinks."

"It's like in Stanley Cup over at the Game Place," Josh said, getting excited and slicking back his red hair. "I know exactly what's on your mind whenever you get the puck."

"We'd be like one big, three-headed, goal-scoring monster!" Woody said. "If we played together, Bradley wouldn't have a chance in the game this afternoon."

"Nobody would be able to stop the Three Musketeers!" Josh exclaimed, standing up and lifting an imaginary sword.

But the truth was, it wasn't up to them. It was up to Coach, and Coach seemed to want Derrick in the goal.

Every day that passed, Derrick was growing more and more frustrated with playing goalie. No matter how many hours he spent practicing the egg drill in his room, he still couldn't keep his other hockey skills sharp. The only way he would ever improve was if he played competitive hockey. That meant playing offense on a strong team in a strong league.

The game that afternoon was at home, against Bradley. It would probably be the toughest team they faced all season, and Coach McKibben gave them a rousing pep talk.

"We've had a tough season so far, men," Coach said. "But all it takes to win is guts and determination. And goals. Coach Simpson, from the eighth grade team, is going to be watching the game today. He may even give you a few pointers. Why don't you show him what you can do? I want you to get out there and play your hearts out."

Coach Simpson was standing next to Coach McKibben, looking over the team with a cool eye. Derrick wondered why the coach of the eighth grade team was suddenly so interested in the seventh graders. But he didn't give it a second thought as the Panthers hit the ice.

Derrick had a great first period. Even from the goal, it was clear that Derrick was the Panthers' star player. He singlehandedly stopped the powerful Bradley offense, making one great save after the other.

Neither team scored in the first period.

At the break, while Derrick was eating an orange, Woody came up and slapped him on the back.

"Great play out there, Derrick," Woody said. "And I'm sure you impressed Coach Simpson."

"What do I care if I impress the eighth grade coach?" Derrick said. "He coaches a bunch of turkeys, no matter how good they are."

"That's true," Woody said. "But don't you see why Coach Simpson is here?"

"For his health?" Derrick answered.

"He's here on a little scouting mission," Woody said. "To check *you* out."

Just then the ref blew his whistle for the second period, and Derrick didn't have time to think about what Woody had said.

Alden's offense picked up during the second period. Woody and Josh and A.J. were playing well together—better than they had all year.

Halfway through the period, Josh stole the puck from the Bradley left winger. He passed to A.J., who was speeding toward the blue line. A.J. took it over the blue line, and then got into trouble with the Bradley defensemen. So he passed it back to Woody, who was speeding in toward the goal. Woody took a wrist shot on goal, but the Bradley goalie made a fine save.

As Derrick sat back in the goal and watched, he wished he could be up with all the action.

But he didn't have a chance to stew about it, because suddenly Bradley stole the puck. The center was skating right toward Derrick in a clean breakaway.

Derrick crouched down and kept his eyes on the puck. He knew that this center liked to fake to the left and then shoot to the right. So he prepared himself to dive.

The center did exactly what Derrick had thought he'd do. He pumped to the left, stopped short, and then fired right. Derrick lunged out and caught the slap shot in his goaltender's glove. Another incredible save.

It was probably the best game of the season for Derrick—even if he *was* in the goal. When the second period was over, the score was still 0–0.

Eight minutes into the third period, there was a big tie-up in Alden's defensive zone. Suddenly the puck came drifting high up in the air toward Derrick. Derrick knew that flip shots were some of the hardest shots to save, because you never knew which way they'd bounce. So he lunged out toward the puck, in order to grab it before it hit the ice, but it took a crazy bounce and trickled past him into the net.

The Bradley team went crazy. There were only two minutes left in the game, and it looked like an easy win.

Coach McKibben called a time-out. The whole team skated over to the sidelines, where Coach McKibben and Coach Simpson were standing.

"We're going to change 'em up, men," Coach said. "Derrick, I want you at center. A.J., you suit up and get into the goal."

Derrick could hardly believe his ears. He was

going to play center! He was so excited he almost ripped the pads off his legs. Josh and Woody slapped him five and the Panthers skated out onto the ice, in high spirits.

Derrick felt great on the ice. But there were only two minutes left and he'd have to work fast.

Derrick dominated the play, and kept the puck in Bradley's defensive zone. He took two shots, but both were a little wide. Time was ticking away.

Woody got a rebound from the goalie's stick and sent it back to Josh, who was speeding in along the left boards. Derrick skated behind Josh and Josh dropped the puck back for him. Derrick had open ice between him and the goal.

Don't screw this up, he thought as he charged forward. *This is your chance to shine.*

Suddenly the goalie charged out of the net toward Derrick, trying to cut down Derrick's angles. Derrick faked right but the goalie wasn't fooled. So he had two options. He could either pass off to Woody, who was out of shooting position, or he could keep on going and try to stickhandle past the goalie.

Derrick decided to keep on going, but he faked like he was going to pass. The goalie bought it and looked away from the net for a split second . . . long enough for Derrick to make a quick wrist shot into the top corner of the net.

Goal!

Derrick lifted his stick up and Josh and Woody came over and congratulated him. It was a spectacular shot, and Derrick felt like a winner.

The score was tied, 1–1.

And that's how the game ended, in a tie. But the Panthers were happy, and everybody was slapping Derrick on the back and giving him high fives. They no longer had a strictly losing record.

"Good work, men," Coach said, beaming. "Bradley is one of the toughest teams in the league. You should be proud. And Derrick, nice shooting."

After the game, Derrick, Josh, and Woody all went out for pizza, to celebrate. Everybody's spirits were soaring. The three friends went over the goal again and again, describing what each of them had done to help.

Derrick was happy about the goal. He was also happy to have such great friends.

"All for one and one for all," Josh exclaimed. "The Three Musketeers strike again!"

9

The next day at practice the whole team was doing Derrick's figure eight drill, and Derrick was leading the way . . . in full goalie gear. No matter how heavy the equipment was, Derrick still outskated everyone with his long, easy strides.

But he was sick and tired of wearing those pads. Yesterday, in the game against Bradley, it had felt so good to take off all that gear, and skate fast again, to shoot the puck, and score a goal. It had felt great to play center, yet Derrick knew that he hadn't played his best hockey. He knew in his heart that his hockey skills had slipped since joining the Alden Panthers.

While they were skating figure eights, everyone noticed that the eighth grade coach had taken a seat next to Coach McKibben. The two coaches were watching the team skate, and discussing something quietly. Derrick could see Coach McKibben nodding his head.

Just then Coach McKibben blew the whistle and the skating stopped. It was time to scrimmage.

Derrick played the first ten minutes of the scrimmage in the goal. He had to admit that he was playing extra hard this afternoon—for the sake of the eighth grade coach. When he fell down on a loose puck, he would jump up quickly to his skates and pass the puck up ice. He used all of his fancy goaltending techniques—the butterfly drop, the pad stack, the kick save, the half splits and the full splits. He caught with his goaltender's glove, and deflected with his stick, too.

But he was tired of being a goalie. He wanted to show Coach Simpson what he could do on the front line.

After the break in the scrimmage, Derrick got his chance. Coach McKibben told him to take off the pads and play center.

Derrick was fired up and ready to go, and it showed

in the way he played. He faced off against Woody. As soon as Coach dropped the puck, Derrick whacked Woody's stick away—just like he had in the very first practice of the season. Then Derrick flipped the puck between Woody's legs, skated around him, and picked it up on the other side. He broke away from the two defensemen with a couple of beautiful fakes, and then all he had to do was beat A.J. Pape at the goal.

Derrick decided to fake to the right, and then shoot for A.J.'s stick side. So he pumped to the right, and A.J. fell for it, leaping way out of position. It was an easy shot and Derrick flicked his stick. But the puck sped two feet to the left of the net. It bounced off the boards and the other team cleared it up ice.

I really have lost my skills, Derrick thought sadly, as he skated toward the puck.

Derrick didn't score for the rest of the scrimmage, either. Nonetheless, he outskated, outpassed, and outshot everyone else on the ice.

When the practice was over, Coach asked Derrick to stay behind for a minute. All his friends left the ice and disappeared into the locker room. Coach Simpson appeared and walked over to Coach McKibben.

"Derrick, this is Coach Simpson, the coach of the

eighth grade team," Coach McKibben said. "Coach
Simpson and I have been doing a lot of talking about
you. We know your skills are far better than anyone
else's on the seventh grade team. And we know that
if a player isn't challenged, he won't improve. So we
think that it might be best for your development to
switch over to the eighth grade team."

"Really?" Derrick said, amazed.

"I've been keeping my eye on you, Derrick, and
I've been very impressed," Coach Simpson added. "I
think the eighth grade team could really benefit from
having you on the roster. And more importantly, I
think *you* could benefit by playing with guys who
are near your level of skill."

Derrick felt his chest swell with pride. He tried
hard to keep himself from breaking into a huge, stupid grin.

"This decision is up to you, Derrick," Coach
McKibben remarked. "I sure would be happy to keep
you here on the seventh grade team. But you should
consider your future as a hockey player, too. It's a
big decision, Derrick. Why don't you sleep on it and
tell me what you've decided tomorrow."

"Thanks, Coach McKibben," Derrick said, beaming. "And thank you, Coach Simpson."

Derrick felt like he was flying as he ran full speed

toward the Game Place. Josh and Woody were waiting there for him—and he couldn't wait to tell them the big news. As he ran through the streets of Cranbrook, he imagined what it would be like to play for the Minnesota North Stars. He pictured himself as the star of the team, scoring goals—maybe even stealing the puck from Gretzky himself. He pictured how all the rest of the North Stars would pile on top of him when he scored the goal that won the Stanley Cup. The whole rink would be screaming and chanting his name.

Suddenly all his dreams seemed possible again. That is, if he moved up to the eighth grade team.

"The eighth grade team?" Josh said, his jaw dropping open. "That bunch of jerks?"

"I saw it coming a mile away," Woody added with a little smile. "Congratulations, Derrick."

The three friends were standing over the Stanley Cup hockey game at the Game Place. Derrick and Josh were in the middle of a game.

"Yeah, I mean congratulations and everything, Derrick," Josh said. "But are you actually going to do it?"

"I think so," Derrick answered, as he worked the little puck up the board. "I really miss competitive play. I think moving up would be good for me."

"You're probably right," Woody said sadly.

"I'll really miss you guys," Derrick said. He took a shot and scored. "But I need a little more competition."

"So I guess this is the end of the Three Musketeers," Josh said. "I guess it's no longer 'All for one and one for all.' "

"Yeah, since the eighth graders practice right after we do, I guess we won't really be seeing very much of you," Woody said.

"I guess not," Derrick said.

Derrick made a great shot and scored again. He was beating Josh at Stanley Cup for the first time in his life. But somehow it really wasn't that much fun. He felt like he already missed Woody and Josh, even though they were standing right next to him. These guys were his best friends. In fact, *all* the guys on the seventh grade team were his friends.

Derrick won the knob hockey game, 10–7.

"Nice game, Derrick," Josh said. "And congratulations on moving up. It'll really help your game."

"Yeah, congratulations," Woody added.

"Hey, why don't we all go over to my house and work on the egg drill?" Derrick said. "My mom made a whole batch of brownies this afternoon."

"Thanks, but I'd better get home," Woody said.

"Me, too," Josh said.

As Derrick walked home alone, he couldn't help but wonder if he was making the right decision. He would miss Woody and Josh and the rest of his friends. He would miss all the fun of Pete's Pizza and the Game Place and the Three Musketeers. Those were the things that made moving to Cranbrook not so bad.

But what about his hockey future? What about the Minnesota North Stars?

One thing was sure. He'd never get to the North Stars if he kept playing on the seventh grade team.

10

"Gentlemen, I want you to meet the newest player on the team," Coach Simpson said the next day at practice. "This is Derrick Larson. Derrick was on the seventh grade team, but Coach McKibben and I thought he needed some stiffer competition. He's a good player and we're lucky to have him."

Derrick's heart was pounding like crazy. He was big for his age, so he was just about the same size as the eighth graders. But for some reason he didn't *feel* as big. It was probably just knowing that these guys were a year older.

"Now, Derrick," Coach Simpson began. "In the eighth grade, we allow body-checking. I know there isn't any body-checking in the seventh grade, but since you're a big kid, I feel confident that you'll do fine. I'm just warning you that the game gets a little rougher."

Derrick nodded. He didn't mind body-checking. He didn't mind playing good rough hockey, as long as it was fair.

"Are you ready for some body checks?" whispered a voice behind him.

Derrick turned around and there was Rothman, staring at him and grinning.

"We hope you don't bruise easy," Petrowsky added, sneering.

Derrick felt like saying, *Hey, you jerks, we're on the same team now,* but he kept his mouth shut.

"I'm going to try Derrick on the front line," Coach said, continuing. "That means Rothman comes out as center, and Derrick goes in. Rothman, you take up left defenseman. Everyone got it? All right. Let's go out there and have a good hard scrimmage."

"Thanks for stealing my position, hotshot," Rothman muttered as they hit the ice.

Derrick could tell from the face-off that the eighth grade team was much better than the seventh grade team. They were all good, fast, two-way skaters.

They could all skate backward as fast as forward.
They could all stickhandle well and check hard. It
felt great to be playing competitive hockey again.

And it felt great to be out of the goal.

Derrick could almost feel his game improving by
the minute. His passes got sharper and his shots
were all on goal. But the goalie was better than
Bannister, and he made some great saves.

Rothman and Petrowsky were the defensemen for
the other team, and Rothman got in some pretty hard
body checks. But Derrick checked him right back.

After a short break, Derrick skated out to center
ice to take the face-off. His opponent was Nick Wilkerson, a fast skater with blond hair and glasses. Derrick decided to go for Wilkerson's stick, and so when
Coach Simpson dropped the puck, Derrick took a
swing. So did Wilkerson, and the two boys scrambled
for the puck, their sticks slapping and poking at each
other like swords in a sword fight. Finally Derrick
flipped the puck to the side, where it was picked up
by one of the guys on his team. Derrick sped forward
toward the blue line, where he picked up a great
pass and crossed into his attacking zone. Petrowsky
came speeding toward him, sweep-checking at the
puck and tying Derrick up so much that he had to
pass to the left winger.

Derrick faked like he was breaking right and instead sped back toward the left, where the winger was getting checked into the boards. The puck broke loose just as he approached, and Derrick picked it up and stickhandled it along the boards.

Just then Rothman came speeding across the ice and landed a powerful body check into Derrick's side. Derrick smashed against the boards and Rothman dug his shoulder into Derrick's back. They battled for the puck which went back and forth between their skates.

"Having fun, Boy Wonder?" Rothman asked, under his breath.

Petrowsky skated up and gave Derrick a solid hip check. Derrick dropped his stick and leaned up against the boards to catch his breath.

"Did the Boy Wonder lose the puck?" Rothman muttered as Petrowsky skated up the ice, stickhandling.

Derrick decided to get back at Rothman and Petrowsky. But he decided to do it by outskating and outshooting them.

A minute later, the right winger headmanned the puck to Derrick and Derrick raced across the blue line, stickhandling. Petrowsky and Rothman were waiting.

Petrowsky rushed forward first and tried to head

Derrick into the boards, but Derrick deked him and changed directions, slipping between Petrowsky and the boards.

Derrick felt the awesome power of puck control. His legs pumped like powerful pistons. Now there was nothing that could stop him from scoring.

Not even Rothman.

Rothman came forward to poke-check Derrick but Derrick tucked the puck in toward his skates and dropped his right shoulder. His shoulder caught Rothman square in the chest and sent Rothman sprawling onto the ice.

Now all he had in front of him was the goal.

Derrick knew that the goalie was expecting a deke. So he gave the goalie exactly what he expected— almost. He faked like he was going to send it to the left, but the goalie didn't move. He knew the goalie was waiting for the pump to the right, so Derrick pumped it back to the left instead.

The goalie made a dive to the right and the puck hit the net.

It was a beautiful goal! Derrick felt his old hockey powers coming back. Coach McKibben was right. All Derrick needed was some good, strong competition.

But none of the guys on his side congratulated him

on his goal. They acted as if Derrick didn't even exist. If he had made that shot on the seventh grade team, Josh and Woody and A.J. and Bannister and Sam and Russell and Alex all would have been cheering and giving him high fives.

He kind of wished all his friends had been there to see it.

Coach blew the whistle and everyone headed to the locker room.

Derrick went into the locker room expecting trouble with Rothman and Petrowsky. But nothing happened. Derrick sat alone on the bench, changing into his street clothes, while the rest of the team sat in a big cluster across the locker room. All the eighth graders were laughing and talking. Once or twice Derrick heard the words "Boy Wonder," and knew that they were talking about him.

Was this his new team? Was he supposed to have fun playing with guys who ignored him? He remembered all the fun he used to have with Josh and Woody in the locker room, after practice. They'd be snapping towels at each other and challenging each other to Stanley Cup over at the Game Place. Bannister would come in and say something funny and everyone would laugh.

Now those days were over.

Before Derrick knew it, the eighth graders had left the locker room, and he was all alone. He hadn't felt this lonely since he'd moved to Cranbrook.

But his hockey skills were improving, weren't they?

11

A few days later, Derrick was walking toward the door of the Cranbrook Municipal Ice Rink when Josh and Woody came out. The seventh grade practice had just ended, and the eighth grade practice was just about to begin.

"Hey, guys," Derrick said, smiling a big smile. "How was practice?"

"You should have been there, Derrick," Josh said, laughing. "Bannister dived for a puck and hit his face on the ice. His face mask cracked in two. Then

A.J. went into the goal and Bannister played center, but his ankles were caving in and he kept on falling down. It was the most hilarious thing."

"Sounds funny," Derrick said, wishing he had been there to see it. "That old Bannister's a pretty funny guy."

"Isn't there anyone like Bannister on the eighth grade team?" Woody asked.

"Some of the guys seem pretty cool, but they act like they don't want me around," Derrick answered. "Don't get me wrong. They're really good players. My skills are getting better with every practice. My shooting and even my skating have improved. But they're not much fun. In fact, they act like I don't even exist."

"Sounds like typical eighth graders," Josh said. His face was turning red with anger just thinking about it. "You know, I really don't like those eighth graders. In fact ... I *hate* even thinking about them."

"Relax, Josh," Woody said. "Don't get yourself all worked up over nothing. Let's go play a few games of Stanley Cup over at the Game Place."

Derrick almost wished he could skip practice and go over to the Game Place with his friends. They could even get the old Three Musketeers back together. But he had work to do, and hockey to play.

As he was saying good-bye to his friends, Rothman and Petrowsky came swaggering up.

"Hey, Larson," they said. "I thought you were on our team now. Why are you hanging out with these pip-squeaks?"

"What pip-squeaks are you talking about, Rothman?" Josh said, stepping forward. His face had turned as red as his hair, and his fists were clenched. Josh didn't like getting pushed around.

"I'm talking about you," Rothman said, with a little smile. "You and your whole lousy pip-squeak team."

"We're better than your team," Josh said suddenly. "We could beat you any day of the week."

"What did I just hear you say?" Rothman asked. He stepped up to Josh and looked down on him. "Did I just hear you say that you seventh graders could beat us any day of the week?"

"That's right, Mr. Big Man," Josh answered. "And I mean what I say."

Just then a bunch of eighth grade players walked up.

"Hey, guys," Rothman called out to them. "This little boy here just challenged us to a match with the seventh grade team. He said the seventh grade team could beat us any day of the week. What do you guys say to that?"

All the eighth graders laughed.

"Let's get out of here, before you get us into trouble," Woody whispered, trying to pull Josh away from the group. But Josh wouldn't budge.

"When do you want to play?" Josh asked persistently. "You name the date."

"Are you crazy, Josh?" Woody whispered. "We'll be slaughtered."

"I said name the date," Josh yelled.

Josh was so mad that Derrick thought he'd see puffs of smoke start coming out of his friend's ears.

Rothman gave a big guffaw and pushed Josh in the chest.

"I'm going to give you one chance to take back your challenge," Rothman said. "Remember that you don't have your superstar player anymore. Your old friend the Boy Wonder, Derrick Larson, is a member of *our* team now."

"I don't care," Josh said. "Are you backing down? Are the big eighth graders scared to play the little seventh graders?"

"We'll play your team," Rothman said, smiling a strange, mean smile. "But if the coaches find out we'll be in trouble. So we'll wait until the season is over. Then we'll show you pip-squeaks who's in charge around here."

"You've got a challenge," Josh said. "We'll play after the postseason county tournament."

Josh and Rothman shook hands on it, and then Josh and Woody hurried off toward the mall—without even saying good-bye to Derrick.

As Derrick walked into the rink with his new team, he couldn't believe what had just happened. Why was Josh such a hothead sometimes? The seventh graders didn't have a *chance* against the eighth graders. It would be a slaughter. And *he* would have to help the eighth graders destroy all his friends on the ice.

"What do you think of the challenge, Boy Wonder?" Rothman said to Derrick in the locker room.

Derrick shrugged.

"Your little friend Josh Bank got a little cocky there, didn't he?" Rothman continued, looking down his nose at Derrick. "We're going to have a great time destroying them, aren't we, Boy Wonder?"

Derrick felt like slugging Rothman in the face. Rothman, and most of the eighth graders, thought they were the coolest players on earth. But they were Derrick's teammates now. If he was going to improve his hockey, he had to try to get along with Rothman and Petrowsky and the whole eighth grade team. So Derrick didn't respond to Rothman's taunts. He only shrugged his shoulders. Rothman threw his head back, laughed, and walked away.

The next afternoon, Derrick played his first game with his new team—and it was the best game he had ever played.

Before the last period was over, Derrick had scored the first hat trick of his life.

The game was away, against North Colby. Derrick started at center, and from the first face-off he felt great on the ice. He couldn't believe what a difference it made to play in a more competitive league. It was almost like magic. He could feel himself improving minute by minute.

His first goal came in the first period. Derrick was back-checking the North Colby left winger, and stole the puck from him. The North Colby defensemen came after him but he headmanned the puck up to Nick Wilkerson who was waiting just in front of the red line. Then Wilkerson headmanned to Derrick and Derrick took the puck into the attacking zone. Instead of charging the net, he stopped at the left point and took a blistering slap shot. The puck slipped in under the goalie's pads.

His second goal was in the second period. Rothman

got a good shot on goal, but the goalie deflected the puck toward the left boards, losing his balance in the process. Derrick got the rebound and made a perfect wrist shot into the corner of the net.

He clinched his hat trick in the last seconds of the game. The Panthers were bunched up in front of the North Colby net, and the ice seemed like a blur of sticks and skates. But Derrick gained possession and made a flip shot through everyone's skates and legs. Since the goalie was screened, the puck bounced into the goal, and the Panthers won the game, 3–0.

Derrick had singlehandedly won the game, and he had scored his first hat trick in the process. The funny thing was, he didn't really feel excited about it. Nick and some of his teammates congratulated him, but most of the eighth graders pretended they had done all the scoring themselves. They ignored him in the locker room.

Derrick couldn't believe that he was depressed after scoring his first-ever hat trick. But he was. It would have been different if he had scored the hat trick for the seventh grade team. All his friends would have lifted him on their shoulders, and then afterward they would have gotten pizza at Pete's. Derrick had to admit, he *really* missed his old friends.

12

When Sunday afternoon came around, Derrick was sitting alone in his bedroom, trying to concentrate on some math homework. But it wasn't working. He kept wondering if all his seventh grade friends were at Black's Pond, having their special Sunday practice without him. He pictured Josh standing up in front of everyone, leading the practice, yelling and screaming and joking around till he was red in the face. He pictured Bannister carrying his chairs across the snowy field for the famous chair drill. He pictured Woody's confident skating style, and A.J. working on his figure eights.

The next thing Derrick knew, he was running through the woods with his skates in his hand. He couldn't believe how much he missed the old team. He just hoped that they were still having their special practices.

When he came to the edge of the woods, Derrick stopped short and a big smile spread across his face. He could see all of his friends on Black's Pond, doing the same chair drill that *he* had taught them.

But he wondered if he would still be welcome . . . especially after Josh's challenge to the eighth grade team. Technically, Derrick was the enemy.

"Hey, look who it is!" Bannister called out, catching sight of Derrick at the edge of the pond.

"It's Derrick!" everyone yelled.

"Hey, everyone," Derrick answered, waving.

"Put on your skates and let's have a scrimmage," Woody said, skating up to Derrick with a big smile. "It sure would be great to play with you again."

"Or are you here to meet the eighth graders?" Josh asked.

"No way," Derrick answered, sitting down to put on his skates. "I'm here to see you guys."

"Then you're not an enemy spy?" A.J. asked, smiling.

"Are you kidding?" Derrick answered, relieved at the warm reception he was getting. "I already know everything about you all anyway."

Derrick stood up and skated onto the pond, feeling great to be with all his friends. It felt like old times.

"Tell me, Derrick," Josh whispered, pulling Derrick aside. "What are the eighth graders planning for the big challenge game? Are they going to play rough? Are they going to cheat?"

"I don't know," Derrick answered. "I don't even really feel like a part of the team."

"Even after your hat trick against North Colby?" Josh said with a big smile.

"You heard about it?" Derrick asked, blushing a little.

"Are you kidding?" Josh said. "Woody and I went out and had a pizza at Pete's in your honor. Congratulations."

"Thanks. Those guys never even said *anything* to me, and I won the game for them." Derrick paused. "Still, they're an awfully good team. We . . . I mean *you* guys really don't have much of a chance. Why did you make that challenge anyway?"

"I don't like being called a pip-squeak, and I don't like the way they're treating you, either," Josh answered. "The whole team has decided to spend extra time practicing so we can actually beat those guys . . . I mean *you* guys."

Just then Woody blew the whistle and the two teams lined up for the scrimmage. Derrick dominated the game, but the seventh graders had really improved. Everyone was skating much better. Their passes were crisp and their shots were on goal. Derrick was having the time of his life . . . even though he could feel his own skating slowing down a little. It was so much fun to be with his old team that he didn't really care if his stickhandling was sloppier than usual.

After the scrimmage was over, everyone was walking off to Pete's for a pizza when Derrick saw the eighth grade team walking toward them. They were carrying their skates and sticks and it looked like they were going to scrimmage.

"Look who it is," Rothman said, when the two groups of boys faced off on the snowy field. "It's the little team that challenged the big team to a game. And they're trying to steal our superstar from us."

"Why don't you guys just get on the pond and play," Woody said, trying to calm things down before they got out of hand.

"We will, we will," Rothman said. "We don't want to get into a fight *before* the big game. But at least give us our Boy Wonder back. Remember, he's part of *our* team now."

All the eighth graders then started toward the pond, and Derrick was left standing with his old friends.

"Well, what are you going to do?" Woody asked.

"I guess I'd better go practice with those guys," Derrick said, without much enthusiasm. "But I sure wish I could go with you guys to Pete's instead."

"We understand," Woody said, hitting Derrick on the back. "Maybe we'll go out to Pete's some other time."

"Yeah. And it was great playing with you again, Derrick," Josh said as the whole group walked away.

Derrick watched them go. He had to admit, it really *was* great to play with his old team again. Even if they weren't as good as his new one.

Derrick turned around and walked toward the pond. As soon as he got to the edge, Rothman skated up to him.

"What are you doing here, Boy Wonder?" Rothman said.

"I thought we were practicing," Derrick answered.

"That's right. *We're* practicing," Rothman remarked. "But *you're* going home. Why don't you take your skates and scram."

"I can't believe you, Rothman—" Derrick began.

He felt like slugging Rothman in the mouth, but he stopped himself. He knew the whole eighth grade team would have been on his back otherwise. So instead of slugging Rothman, Derrick turned around to catch his friends—but they had already disappeared.

Derrick walked home alone through the woods, thinking about Josh, Woody, and the other guys, the two teams, and the big challenge game . . . and his hockey future.

Mr. Larson was standing in the kitchen, peeling potatoes for dinner, when Derrick walked in to get some milk.

"Why are you looking so glum, Derrick?" Mr. Larson asked.

"I don't know, Dad," Derrick answered. "I thought it would be a really great thing to be on the eighth grade team. My hockey has gotten a lot better, but . . ."

"But you're not having very much fun?" Mr. Larson said.

"No, I'm not." Derrick took a big gulp of milk. "Sometimes I wish I was back on the old team, with all of my friends. But then my hockey skills would suffer."

"What's more important to you, Derrick," Mr. Larson asked. "Your hockey or your friends?"

Derrick didn't know what to say. He knew what he *felt*, but . . . was that the right thing to feel?

"I don't know, Dad," Derrick said. "What do you think?"

"I think you've got lots of years ahead of you to worry about your hockey," Mr. Larson began. "What good are hockey skills if you don't have any friends?"

That's exactly what Derrick felt. Suddenly a huge weight had been lifted from his shoulders.

"I agree, Dad," Derrick said, smiling. "I had time to think about things this afternoon, and I think I've made up my mind. Tomorrow, I'm going to ask Coach McKibben if I can come back to the seventh grade team."

"I think that's a very mature decision," Mr. Larson said, smiling. He extended his arm and shook Derrick's hand, giving his son a little wink.

Derrick couldn't believe how happy he suddenly felt. Not only could he be with his friends again, but he could help them against the eighth graders in the big challenge game.

Maybe with Derrick's help, the seventh graders wouldn't be totally destroyed.

13

The next day, Derrick showed up early for practice—early enough to watch his old team finishing up their scrimmage. He sat in the stands where no one could see him, and silently cheered on his friends. Woody was playing better than ever. Josh had improved his backward skating, and was passing well. Even Bannister looked better—at least his ankles weren't caving in when he skated. And A.J. looked great in the goal, doing kick saves, half splits, and even a butterfly drop. A.J. made some saves that Derrick wondered if he could have made himself.

Yet if there was one thing that Derrick *didn't* miss, it was being in the goal. In fact, he hoped he never had to put on another set of goalie's pads for the rest of his life. He was an offense man, and he loved the thrill of power-skating and taking blistering slap shots. Playing center had been the best part of being on the eighth grade team.

But if Coach McKibben and Coach Simpson let him go back to the seventh grade team, Derrick didn't care what position he played. He would prefer to play center ... but if Coach McKibben wanted him to go back in the goal, then he would do it.

Watching his friends scrimmage only made Derrick more certain. He wanted to be down there with them, laughing and skating—and afterward go to the Game Place. He just hoped that Coach McKibben and Coach Simpson would see it his way.

When Coach blew the whistle to signal the end of practice, Derrick waited for the team to leave the ice. Then he walked down to Coach McKibben.

"Hey, Coach," Derrick said.

Coach McKibben turned around and a big smile spread across his face.

"Hey, there, Derrick. How are things on the new team?"

"Well . . ." Derrick began. "You were right about moving up to an older team. My hockey has improved a lot."

"I know," Coach McKibben said. "I heard about your hat trick against North Colby. That's great hockey."

"Thanks, Coach," Derrick answered. He took a deep breath and continued, his heart racing in his chest. "But I've come to the decision that some things are more important than my hockey skills. Like loyalty, and being with my friends."

Derrick turned bright red. He felt sort of silly, and hoped that Coach wouldn't think he was "soft" or anything.

"Aren't the guys on the eighth grade team treating you okay?" Coach McKibben asked. "Especially after you singlehandedly won the game against North Colby?"

"They either pretend I don't exist or they call me the Boy Wonder," Derrick answered. "I'm sick and tired of it. If they keep it up I'll end up slugging one of them. So, anyway, Coach, I wonder if I could come back to the seventh grade team."

"I sure would like to have you back," Coach

McKibben said. "But I have to talk to Coach Simpson about it. You're sure you want to do it?"

"I'm sure," Derrick answered.

"Okay. I'll talk to Coach Simpson right now, before the eighth grade practice starts," Coach McKibben said, winking at Derrick. "I'm sure he'll have an answer for you by the end of your practice. Now go ahead and get suited up."

In the locker room, all the eighth graders were talking about the big challenge match with the seventh graders.

"It's going to be a total slaughter," Rothman said as he laced his skates. "None of those guys has ever done any body-checking. We'll be able to hip-check them off the pond like they were little girls. Isn't that right, Boy Wonder?"

"Don't be so sure about it, Rothman," Derrick muttered. "And stop calling me Boy Wonder."

"Well, well," Rothman said, standing up. "Boy Wonder is getting a little bit cocky, just like his old teammates. Too bad you'll have to help in the slaughter of your old friends."

"Listen, Rothman, what do you have against me?" Derrick asked, standing up and looking Rothman squarely in the eye. He had had just about enough of Rothman. "What did I ever do to you?"

"I don't like little pip-squeaks coming in and stealing my position," Rothman said, taking a step closer to Derrick till their noses almost touched. "*I* was the center of this team until you came along."

Both boys were clenching their fists.

"I'm sorry that I'm so much better than you," Derrick answered.

Rothman's face turned red.

"Why don't we step outside right now and have a little talk about that?" Rothman said, pushing Derrick in the chest.

Derrick wanted nothing more than to give Rothman the beating of his life. But he knew that fighting made the coaches mad. And if the coaches were mad, maybe they would make him stay on the eighth grade team.

So Derrick turned around and walked toward the locker room door.

"That wimp won't even fight me," Rothman called out to Derrick's back. "The big superstar is a big wimp."

During the long, hard practice, Derrick looked at Coach Simpson a few times. He could tell that Coach had made up his mind, but Derrick had to wait until practice was over before he learned what the decision was to be.

Coach Simpson came into the locker room and banged his clipboard against the lockers to get everyone's attention.

"Listen up, men," he began. "I've made a decision. Derrick Larson has asked to be moved back down to the seventh grade team. We're going to miss Derrick out there on the ice, but if that's what Derrick wants to do, then that's what will happen. So everyone say good-bye to Derrick. This will be his last practice with us."

"Thanks, Coach!" Derrick shouted.

Coach Simpson gave Derrick a smile and left the locker room.

Derrick felt so happy he thought he might fly out of the locker room. He was going back to his friends! He stuffed his practice uniform into his gym bag and got up to run home and tell his parents the great news.

Rothman stood in his way.

"The Boy Wonder can't handle playing in the big leagues, can he?" Rothman said, standing right in front of Derrick. "He has to go running back to his little pip-squeak friends."

"Listen, Rothman," Derrick said, stepping closer. "Us little pip-squeaks are going to whip you guys in the challenge game. We'll have the last laugh. Just you wait and see."

"Those are big words, Boy Wonder," Rothman said, giving Derrick a forceful push in the chest.

That was the last straw. Derrick pulled his arm back and slugged Rothman in the stomach. Rothman doubled over and then straightened up, swinging wildly. He hit Derrick in the cheek, but Derrick was so mad he didn't feel a thing. He just wound up and slugged Rothman in the nose. Rothman fell down across the bench, holding his face and crying.

"Any other big boys care to fight?" Derrick asked, gazing around the locker room with his fists clenched.

Nobody said a word.

"None of you big bad eighth graders wants to take a swing at me?" Derrick asked again. He couldn't believe what he was saying. But right then, he felt like he could beat up Mike Tyson.

The eighth graders just looked at him.

"Hey, Petrowsky, you better call Rothman's mommy and tell her that her baby has a bloody nose," Derrick said, laughing as he turned to leave. "And I'll see the rest of you guys at the challenge match."

14

"Welcome back!" Josh yelled the next afternoon, as he sat down beside Derrick in the lunchroom. "Everybody heard the news this morning!"

"Thanks, Josh," Derrick answered, flashing a big smile. "Are we going to have a great second half of the season, or what?"

"You said it," Josh remarked, slapping Derrick's back so hard that Derrick almost choked on his potato chips. "With you back on the team, we stand a chance of winning at least a few games."

99

Woody and Bannister walked up with their lunches.

"Look who's here to save our season!" Bannister exclaimed. "It's the Minnesota Kid."

Bannister reached into his lunch bag and pulled out an enormous sandwich, stuffed with ham and beef, hard-boiled eggs and bacon, lettuce and cheese. He handed the sandwich to Derrick.

"I'd like to present you with a very groovy gift—one of my mom's special Tower of Power sandwiches—as a token of our esteem," Bannister began, as if he were handing out an award. "I think I speak for the whole seventh grade hockey team when I say welcome back. And congratulations on giving Rothman a bloody nose."

"You guys heard about that already?" Derrick asked, pushing the Tower of Power sandwich back toward Bannister.

"Are you kidding?" Woody said, punching Derrick in the shoulder. "You're not only a regular Wayne Gretzky, you're also a regular Mike Tyson. Nice going, champ."

"He deserved it," Derrick said. "I'd been waiting all week to slug that guy."

"But, to tell you the truth, Derrick," Woody began, sitting down and taking out his sandwich. "The fact that you beat up Rothman is not going to make our job any easier. I'll bet the whole eighth grade team is going to be out for blood at our big challenge match."

"We'll just have to outsmart them," Derrick said. "We have five games left, and then the postseason county tournament. If we work hard enough in the time we have, and really improve, I think we can beat those guys."

"That's the spirit!" Josh exclaimed.

"Let's just worry about beating Lincoln this afternoon," Woody said. "And let's hope that Coach puts Derrick in at center."

"Then it would be the Three Musketeers, leading the Panthers to victory!" Josh said, lifting up his arm as if he held a sword.

Derrick and Woody lifted their arms, too.

"All for one and one for all!" they all exclaimed together, laughing and smiling while Bannister applauded.

When the game came around, Coach put Derrick in at center. That meant that he and Woody and Josh were the three forwards. The spirit of the Alden Panthers was soaring as they took the ice against their arch rivals, Lincoln . . . with Derrick in the lead.

Not only did Derrick have the time of his life playing with his friends, but he also had the *game* of his life.

He felt like he was flying on his skates. He knew Woody and Josh so well that he could tell when Josh was in trouble, or when Woody wanted to give and go. The Three Musketeers had never played a more beautiful game—and the Lincoln team couldn't believe what was happening.

After the first period, the score was Alden 2, Lincoln 0.

Russell Schultz scored one of the goals, on a fine wrist shot from just outside the crease, and Woody scored the other, on a blazing slap shot from the blue line. Derrick didn't mind that he hadn't scored himself, since he had assisted on both of the goals.

The Panthers kept rolling right through the second period, adding one more goal to the scoreboard, when Josh pushed the puck in during an Alden power play. Lincoln scored two goals of their own, to bring the score to 3–2.

But the third period was all Derrick's. He was like a demon on the ice, and nobody could stop him. All Josh and Woody had to do was get the puck to him, and Derrick would take care of the rest.

Early in the game, Derrick had psyched the goalie

out with his aggressive playing. Now, whichever way Derrick faked, the goalie would jump, and all Derrick had to do was take potshots at the net. He stickhandled like a pro, leaving the defensemen to trip on their own skates. By the time the buzzer rang at the end of the game, Derrick had scored a total of four goals.

Alden had won its first game, 7–2.

The team went nuts, and lifted Derrick up on their shoulders.

"Welcome back!" they all cried.

Even Coach McKibben gave Derrick a high five.

After the game, the locker room was filled with the sound of banshee cries and whistles and cheers. Derrick felt like they had just won the Stanley Cup. He knew then that he had made the right decision by leaving the eighth grade team.

Afterward, Derrick, Josh, and Woody all went out to Pete's for a pizza. As they sat in their usual booth, the three friends recounted all of their goals.

"I liked your slap shot from the blue line," Derrick said to Woody. "You looked just like Gretzky. That goalie didn't know what hit him."

"No, no," Woody said, taking a bite of pizza. "Your *fourth* goal was the best. Remember how I head-manned the puck to you and you faked the defenseman and then skated sideways toward the goal? And then you faked like you were taking a flip shot toward the right corner, but instead you went by the goal and backhanded it into the left corner? That was pure hockey *genius!*"

"Do you know which goal of Derrick's was *my* favorite?" Josh asked, smiling and taking a gulp of soda. "It was the flip shot that went in right above the goalie's shoulder. Remember how it just floated there in the air, nice and slow, but the goalie couldn't do a *thing* about it? That was the *greatest!*"

"The Three Musketeers strike again!" Derrick exclaimed.

"And I get the feeling that the Panthers will be having a great second half of the season," Woody remarked. "I think we've turned this team around. Thanks to you, Derrick."

Derrick blushed and gave a little shrug.

"Don't compliment him *too* much," Josh said, with a glimmer in his eye. "If he gets an inflated ego, I'll just have to cream him in a game of Stanley Cup at the Game Place."

"Is that a challenge, Mr. Bank?" Derrick asked.

"You bet it is, Mr. Larson," Josh responded.

A few minutes later, they were all at the Game Place, playing arcade hockey and talking about the rest of the season.

15

The rest of the season was better than anyone expected—in fact, it seemed almost like a miracle. The Alden Panthers came back from a dismal record of 0–6–1, to end up with a final record of 6–6–1. Beginning with the game against Lincoln, the Panthers seemed to catch fire and play at the top of their abilities. The team spirit was soaring, and their skills were sharpening with every game. It seemed like the Panthers couldn't lose.

And Derrick Larson led the way.

Teams like St. Stephen's, North Colby, and South

Colby seemed to roll over and die when the Panthers came onto the ice. Derrick added two more hat tricks to his season, and even Woody scored three goals against the weak St. Stephen's squad. But the toughest game by far was the last game of the season—a rematch against Williamsport.

Williamsport had been the first team the Panthers played that season, and the Panthers wanted to show them how much they had improved.

The Williamsport team had improved as well, and the competition on the ice was fierce. Early in the game, Josh was called for high-sticking and spent two minutes in the penalty box. The Williamsport team went on the power play, and worked the puck toward the crease. Just when the Panthers had tied up the puck, Williamsport passed out to their defenseman at the point, who made a beautiful slap shot that slipped under A.J.'s pads. The first period ended with Alden down by a goal.

During the second period, the defense ruled. Each team had one or two shots on goal—and that was all. The rest of the time the defense jammed up the offense with poke checks and sweep checks.

The third period started out just the same. Time was running out and Alden was still down 1–0. With only twenty seconds left in the game, Derrick stole the puck from the Williamsport center. He sped up the left boards, past the Williamsport defenseman, and over the attacking blue line. The ice was wide open and Derrick knew he couldn't fail.

The whole game depends on this shot, Derrick thought as he sped forward.

Derrick lifted his stick and slapped the puck toward the goalie's stick side. It was a picture-perfect shot, and the goalie ended up on his rear, hitting his stick in anger against the ice. The seventh grade team cheered and screamed and nearly mauled Derrick with joy.

The game went into sudden-death overtime.

The death was sudden indeed. Derrick was still pumped up from his goal when he went up to the face-off circle at center ice. He won the face-off, got the puck out to Woody, and broke up ice. Woody headmanned the puck and Derrick slapped it right into the left side of the net. The whole thing took about five seconds.

Alden had won, and the regular season ended.

Now the Panthers began to get psyched up for the big game against the eighth grade team. They held a special Sunday practice at Black's Pond where Derrick warned them that the eighth graders planned to play rough, that their sheer size and strength would make them dominate the game. So Derrick taught everyone how to body-check. They spent the day working on hip checks and shoulder checks, as well as agility and stickhandling drills. Derrick knew that the seventh graders could never over-power the eighth graders, but they just might be able to outsmart, and out*spirit* them.

But before the big challenge match, the Panthers had to go through the postseason, county-wide tour-nament held in the large rink at the state university, an hour's bus ride away. The only problem was, they were getting so psyched up for the challenge match that they almost didn't care about the official tour-nament.

Luckily their first match was against St. Ste-phen's, the weakest team in the league, and the Panthers won, 1–0.

"We won, men," Coach McKibben said in the locker room after the game. "But only by a hair. What was the problem out there? It seemed like you guys had something else on your minds."

Coach McKibben was exactly right. The whole team was thinking about the eighth grade challenge match.

It all caught up with them in the next tournament game, which was against Williamsport. Williamsport was out for revenge for their defeat, and they just plain outplayed the Panthers. The game was good, but the Panthers lost 3–1.

"We had a fine season, men," Coach McKibben said in the locker room afterward. "We started off a little rough, but we picked ourselves up by the bootstraps and showed the league what we were really made of. I'm proud of each and every one of you guys. Each player on the team has worked hard and improved. You should all be proud of a great season."

Everyone stood and gave Coach a round of applause.

"I think we should take that good spirit and give it to the eighth grade team," Coach added, while everyone was still clapping. "They're playing in the finals of the tournament right now. Anyone who can, should go out there and cheer the older team on to victory."

Suddenly everyone was completely silent.

"What's wrong?" Coach asked. "I don't hear much support for the eighth graders. Where's your school spirit?"

"Sorry, Coach," Derrick said at last, winking in secret to Josh and Woody. "We promise to go out and watch the game."

A few minutes later, Derrick, Josh, Woody, and A.J. were sitting in the crowded bleachers, watching the eighth graders play in the tournament final.

"I have to admit, they look pretty darn good," Woody remarked.

"And pretty darn *big*," A.J. added.

"What are you wimps talking about?" Josh exclaimed, punching Woody in the shoulder. "We have to keep our spirit up. We can beat those guys, no problem."

"Well, South Colby is sure having a problem beating them, and they're the best team in the eighth grade league," A.J. remarked.

"I hope Alden wins," Derrick said.

"What?!" Josh exclaimed, spinning his head to Derrick. "Did you just say what I thought you said?"

"I said I hope Alden wins," Derrick repeated. "Because if they win, they'll be so cocky that they won't take the challenge match seriously. Then we'll be able to surprise them, and clobber them before they know what's happening."

Josh nodded thoughtfully.

"Keep your eyes open, guys," Derrick continued. "Learn what each of the eighth graders plays like."

The seventh graders sat in silence, concentrating on the game. They watched how Rothman skated, and which side Petrowsky liked to shoot from.

The eighth graders went on to win the game, and the county championship. Everyone poured out onto the ice and there were whistles whistling and horns blowing. The eighth graders were screaming and yelling in celebration.

"Hey, Derrick," Woody said, as they were riding on the bus back toward Cranbrook. "If you had stayed on the eighth grade team, you'd be an all-county champion right now. You'd have another big trophy to put on your dresser."

"I know," Derrick answered, as he taped his stick.

"Are you sorry you came back to play with us pip-squeaks?" Woody asked.

"Are you kidding?" Derrick said. "It was the best decision of my life. There'll be lots of other championships."

"Like the challenge match against the eighth graders," Woody said.

"Exactly," Derrick responded. "If we can win *that* game, it will be the biggest championship I can think of."

The challenge match was that Sunday, at Black's Pond.

16

Sunday was a cold, bright day. A few white clouds hung in the blue sky, and Black's Pond looked very calm and peaceful at the edge of the snowy field. It was almost *too* calm and peaceful . . . like a battle-field before the battle begins.

At around noon the two teams began to gather on opposite sides of the pond. They talked quietly among themselves, getting ready for the game.

"Okay, men," Derrick said to the seventh grade team assembled before him. "This is the big game. It's going to be a rough one. When things get *really* rough, just remember what I said. We can't outpower the eighth graders, but we *can* out*smart* them. We just have to stickhandle well and remember to deke and pass. We have to back-check and fore-check aggressively. And when we can, we have to body-check. You'd better believe they're going to be body-checking us as much as they can. We can beat these guys. I played on their team, and I know what I'm talking about."

"Did you hear what Rothman said at school on Friday?" Josh called out. "He said that there wasn't a chance in the world that the county champion team could lose to a bunch of seventh graders."

"See?" Derrick said, pointing his stick across the ice at the other team. "They think they own the world. That means they're going to be lazy out there. That means they think they'll be able to skate all over us. But we have two things that they will *never* have. Guts and spirit."

Everyone stood up and put their sticks together like they were swords.

"Guts and spirit!" they all cried.

Just then the referee blew the whistle. He was the center from the high school team. Rothman and his teammates had asked him to referee the game, and Derrick was worried that he wouldn't be fair.

The starting twelve skated out onto the ice.

"We're not playing an official game," the ref called out, "so the rules won't be quite as tight. I expect some hard checking. I expect to see some *real* hockey. Everybody understand?"

The two teams got ready for the face-off. Derrick watched Rothman skate up toward the center of the pond. He hadn't seen Rothman since he slugged him in the nose.

"Well, if it isn't the Boy Wonder," Rothman said, as he stopped and sprayed Derrick with ice. "I want you to know something, Boy Wonder. I don't forget easily."

"Neither do I, Rothman," Derrick said, staring square into Rothman's eye.

The ref dropped the puck and Rothman went for Derrick's stick. The puck scooted out between their legs and was picked up by Justin Johnson, the eighth grade left winger. Derrick skated off after Johnson, but a second later felt a huge blow on his side and fell flat on the ice.

Rothman had given Derrick a hip check when Derrick didn't even have the puck! That was unnecessary roughness if he had ever seen it! Rothman should have gotten two minutes in the penalty box for that. But the ref didn't blow his whistle.

Derrick scrambled back to his feet and skated off

toward the action—but he had bruised his hip when he hit the ice and now it hurt to skate. As he was skating toward his defensive zone, he saw Petrowsky give Josh a nasty hip check that sent Josh flying into the reeds at the edge of the pond. A second later, Johnson gave Russell Schultz a shoulder check that laid him flat.

Since none of them had the puck, it was all completely illegal.

Derrick felt his blood begin to boil.

So this is what they want to play like, he thought. *It doesn't surprise me a bit.*

A moment later, three of the five seventh grade players had been body-checked and were struggling to get up from the ice. Rothman had the puck and he deked Alex Kroll and then sent a slap shot into the goal before Derrick could check him.

All the eighth graders cheered, and skated back toward center ice for the next face-off.

Derrick called a conference over by the edge of the pond.

"Okay, guys, this is going to be even rougher than I thought," Derrick whispered. "But we need to fight back. We need to be quicker than they are. We need to duck out of their body checks. And I, for one, plan to body-check Rothman to kingdom come."

115

"We have only just begun to fight," Josh said.

Josh's face was turning red. So was Derrick's. So was Woody's. They were ready to play.

At the next face-off, Rothman went for Derrick's stick again but Derrick lifted it and stole the puck. He passed it out to Woody who broke away down ice, toward the eighth grade goal. Woody passed to Josh who was hip-checked by Rothman. Josh went flying into the reeds again, and Rothman took the puck up ice.

Derrick's hip was still bruised, but he didn't feel it anymore. He had only one thing on his mind.

Body-checking Rothman.

He skated alongside Rothman for a moment, poke-checking at the puck, and then he eased away a few feet . . . a few feet were all he needed to get his momentum up.

He laid his shoulder right into Rothman's side with all his strength, sending Rothman flying off the pond. Rothman landed face first in a bank of snow and Derrick heard the whole seventh grade team let out a huge roar.

But he didn't have time to enjoy the applause. Instead, Derrick grabbed the loose puck and sped down toward the eighth grade goal. The defensemen were charging in to check him, but just as Petrowsky was about to send his shoulder into Derrick's side, Derrick changed speed and Petrowsky went sliding past him. Derrick passed the puck to Woody, who was just in front of the crease, and Woody ragged it until Derrick skated into better position. When Derrick got the pass from Woody he lifted his stick and took a slap shot.

The puck went into the top right corner of the net.

The seventh grade team went crazy. The score was all tied up, 1–1.

Derrick's goal gave the seventh graders the extra bit of spirit they needed. Derrick scored another goal right away, and then Woody scored one at the end of the period.

So after the first period, the score was 3–1.

The second period was every bit as rough as the first. Everyone on the seventh grade team had bruises all over their bodies—but they didn't care one bit. All they cared about was getting the puck into the eighth grade net.

And that's exactly what they did. Derrick scored once, on a slap shot from the far edge of the pond. And then Josh scored on a beautiful backhand shot from just outside the crease.

The eighth graders got a lot of shots on goal, but A.J. was playing brilliantly. He made catches and saves that brought the seventh grade team cheering to its feet. And he didn't let one goal slip past him.

At the end of the second period, the score was 5–1.

Derrick could see the surprise on the eighth graders' faces. Here they were—the eighth grade county champions—being slaughtered by a bunch of pip-squeak seventh graders. By the time the third period was halfway through, the eighth graders had lost their heart. They stopped body-checking and took wild slap shots from the middle of the ice. One time, Rothman tripped on his own skates and went sprawling across the pond.

Even as the eighth grade team gave up, the seventh grade team grew more and more fierce. They weren't about to let up on the pressure for a second. Even Bannister played well.

In fact, it was Bannister who got the loudest cheer that afternoon, when he gave Petrowsky such a huge hip check that Petrowsky flew into the air and landed ten feet away. It took Petrowsky so long to get up from the ice that Bannister stood beside him and took a bow, as the seventh graders cheered like crazy.

Derrick expected the whole eighth grade team to charge onto the ice from the edge of the pond—and then the game would have ended in a huge fight.

But it seemed the eighth graders had even lost the heart for that.

When the ref blew the whistle at the end of the game, the score was seventh grade 8, eighth grade 1!

The whole team rushed onto the ice and everyone was hugging each other and cheering.

It was the greatest victory of Derrick's life, greater than any county championship. It was even greater than all the championships he had won back in Minnesota.

Suddenly Derrick felt himself being lifted up onto his best friends' shoulders.

"Great game, Derrick!" Josh cried.

"We couldn't have done it without you!" Woody exclaimed.

"The Minnesota Kid strikes again," Bannister shouted.

Derrick Larson had never been happier in his whole life.